The Nightingale Files:
The Rook and Queen

THE NIGHTINGALE FILES:
THE ROOK AND QUEEN

Megaphone Publishing

Copyright © 2015 Megan Meredith

Cover Photography: Sydney Abbott
Cover design by Tim Logan Art

Editing by HG Editing
Chapter illustrations Tim Logan Art
Author photograph by Tawni Tuckfield

ISBN: 0692925902

ISBN-13:978-0692925904

To my proofreaders; Robin, Kyle, Sarah, and Brit—thank you for being my other sets of eyes. Thank you for seeing things differently than me and believing enough in me to share your opinions.

To my beautiful cover model, Maddie—thank you for letting me use your beauty to portray AB!

Tim—your talents and artistry never cease to blow me away. Thanks for coming on this journey with me once again. I am so thankful to know you and have your covers on my books.

Si—thank you for your expertise in all things football, coaching and juvenile.

To my readers (however few you may be...)—thank you for reading, for always coming back for more, and for inviting me to book clubs, writing reviews, and sticking with me as I learn and grow.

1.

NEVER UNDERESTIMATE THE POWER OF A WELL-PLACED ROOK

"Didn't you iron your uniform?" Mother asked as she plated my sausage and eggs and set them in front of me.

I nodded, still trying to pry my eyelids closer to my wide, blonde eyebrows.

"It's the first day of school, Avery Brave," she added, scolding me sweetly as only a southern mamma can do.

"Yes, Mother, I know." Taking a sip from my coffee, I wondered why she was so snippy this morning.

Her short, blonde, pixie hair was always styled perfectly, and her makeup was always on point, including bold lipstick that looked ravishing against her perfect complexion. This morning, however, I could see tired eyes and dark circles beneath her mascara.

"Gracious, Avery. I don't mean to be negative, but you worry me. You should try to care, at least a little."

"Mom, please. I'm not awake yet. And it's just high school," I said around the sausage in my mouth, knowing that would irritate her further. *Anyway,* I thought cynically, *I think we're well past caring what people think of me.*

"Avery, don't talk with your mouth full. At least fix your hair. I'll meet you in the car," she dictated as she disappeared to her room.

First day of school. I should have gone to bed earlier. I should have bought a new backpack. I should have gotten my hair cut, eyebrows shaped, or nails shellacked like the other girls do. But I didn't. My hair was almost white in streaks from the sun, curly and generally untamed. My nails were cut short, and my fresh face was tan and filled with freckles from a summer by the pool. I figured that, if the kids at All Saints Academy didn't like me the way I was, then I didn't care if they liked me at all.

But this year, that would be easier said than lived, because my best friend, Carol, had moved over the summer to Colorado. I had stayed up till 2 a.m. Facetiming with her when I should have been asleep, and now, my eyes were puffy, and my hair was a mess, and Mother disapproved of to slightly rumpled collar of my white button-up shirt neatly tucked inside my navy vest. Probably a half an inch of it showed, but Mother would say that half an inch was a disgrace.

Oh well. Disgrace it is.

The end of summer in the Ozarks was as duplicitous as any other season. There was a certain bipolar swinging that occurred from day to day. One could never be certain what was the appropriate clothing, and, oftentimes, one would need several options; it would be cold and rainy in the morning and sweltering by afternoon or pleasantly spring-like in the morning and snowy in the evening. It had rained a lot in June, which kept everything bright green all summer even though the heat was at record index highs, and all our pools would be open until well into September.

Bentonville was busy in the mornings, but traffic on the first day of school was a special kind of ridiculous. I'd be sixteen in three weeks, but until then, Mother would to drive me to school in the mornings. I had told her I could ride my bike, but she'd insisted, and I'd eventually conceded.

She's always been too peppy in the mornings and slightly judgmental, but mostly that's because I'm not awake yet. This morning, as we got into the car and headed out, she was on edge and less peppy, but I assumed it was the same reason that I felt apprehensive about starting back to school. I watched our sprawling two-story house—really more of an estate, if I'm honest—slowly shrink in the rearview mirror as we pulled out of the subdivision. The property was rather excessive for just the three of us, and I always thought it was secretly wasteful, but I did enjoy our pool.

The columns on the front veranda reached high and arched toward each other. Mother's love for gardening and plants showed in the meticulous landscaping and perfectly southern hanging florals.

"I know you've been out for a long time," Mother spoke up as she pulled to a stop in front of my school, "and this year will be hard without Carol, so I'm praying for you to make a new friend, even today."

"Thanks, Mom," I muttered, irritated that she'd brought up last year and Carol right before I got out of the car. *But she means well,* I scolded myself. I managed to give her a sincere smile and remind her that I'd be working on the paper after school and that Dad could pick me up.

As I walked toward the entrance of All Saints Academy, I repeated to myself, *This is only high school.* I naively hoped that maybe this year would be better than last year. *Probably anything would be better than last year.*

Mother always told me that the relationships she made in high school were lifelong. That usually makes me groan, because I never signed up to know *these* people my whole life. That was done by my parents.

Though there were a few people that I didn't despise—like the librarian who had written several books and taught underprivileged children how to read on the weekends at the county library. There was Ms. Milder, too, the guidance counselor who seemed keenly aware of good music trends and had tattoos, though I'm sure I wasn't supposed to know that. And lastly, there was my newspaper teacher, Mr. Knight, who was brooding and sarcastic but always encouraged me to seek out the real story and find a new angle. Most girls talked about him as the most attractive teacher at our private Christian school, but I found it disturbing that they didn't see the irony in that line of thinking.

Inside the grand front doors, my radar, which Mother always says will be the death of me, was firing on all cylinders. The prettiest girls were to my left with the heavy-lifters sidled up next to them; the technos were across the lobby, busy talking about the latest brilliant gadget, while the overachievers were super-serious, ambitious, and full of self-discipline, waiting quietly for the doors to open. These weren't technical terms, or even terms others would know, of course; they were just labels that Carol and I had given a few of the cliques at All Saints.

There were plenty more, but, before I started cataloguing all their first-day nuances, I spotted a boy I'd never seen before. If he had any insecurities, they were nicely masked by the "I hate this place already" look on his chiseled face. His dark, expertly cut hair and large brown eyes topped off his tall, lanky build.

Mysterious ambiguity, I assessed to myself. He put in his earbuds and effectively shut everyone out. *Who is he, and how did he have the misfortune to come to be here?* I jokingly wondered to myself. *Transferring into Saints is hard business.*

He was already doing a fine job just being aloof. I wished I could be more like him, and the thought of it made me smile.

And a smile was pretty good progress for my first day of high school.

I tried for the third time to get my locker to lock. It was like cracking a safe getting it open in the first place, and now it wouldn't close. I yanked all my books out and huffed up to the front office and instantly retracted my thoughts about progress. This was shaping up to be the worst first day of school ever. I missed Carol, my prime-real-estate locker was broken, and on top of that, Mr. Knight had already stopped me in the hall to tell me I was covering the first pep rally and game, which was Friday night. Pep is not really my thing.

"I need a new locker; #733 is broken," I announced a little too loudly when I reached the desk in the main office.

"I'm sorry, Ms...."

"Nightingale."

"I'm sorry, Ms. Nightingale. Let's see if we can get you a new one," the mousy brunette with glasses said behind her computer. "Oh my," she added as she squinted at her screen.

"Oh my what?" I asked, both annoyed and concerned.

"Well, it appears we only have one locker left. It's #1."

"#1 is the very last locker! I'll be late."

"Technically, it's the very first locker. And, well, Ms. Nightingale, you're already late."

"I know, but I'll be late to every class! Every day! Can't you get my locker fixed?"

"I'm afraid it will take a while to get it looked at. In the meantime, you can have #1. Here's a note to get you to class."

"Thanks," I muttered, trudging out of the office and down the halls until I reached what seemed like the very last corner of the very last hall in the school.

The new kid with the dark hair and the earbuds squatted down at the bottom locker underneath mine. *So, I guess it's not the very worst. At least I got the top.*

I slowed up, hoping the kid would finish so I wouldn't have to reach over him. He looked up and saw me coming.

"Hey," he said, giving me a nod of acknowledgement.

"Hey," I said back. "Guess I'm not the only one sentenced to the back corner." I squelched butterflies in my stomach at talking to someone I didn't know.

"What'd you do to deserve this?" His mouth slid into a smirk, revealing a dimple on his left cheek and impossibly straight teeth. "I'm new. I assumed the worst locker was part of initiation."

"My luck is *just* that good. I had a great spot, but it was broken. So, I traded up for this." I posed like Vanna White turning over a letter, realizing I was acting either completely neurotic or inappropriately comfortable with this new kid. Either way, he laughed.

"Nice." He stood and moved out of the way so I could get to #1 but didn't leave. "My name is Felix." He smiled and, to my surprise, actually extended his hand to shake mine. "Felix Rook."

"Nice to meet you, Felix. I'm Avery Brave Nightingale."

"All one word?"

"No, not really. It's two words, but it's my whole name nonetheless."

"Why use both?"

"Parents decided it."

He nodded as though he understood what I was implying. "I like it. Avery Brave," he repeated. "It's cool."

"Thanks."

I closed my locker, and we started walking together down the hall.

"Can I walk with you?" he asked. "Or is that creepy?"

My butterflies had dissolved, and I realized that I wasn't nervous. I nodded once. "I used to go here, but I've been out for a while. So, we'll be new kids together."

He did a small fist pump in the air and nodded. "Things are looking up."

"What do you have first track?" I asked.

"Spanish, then English."

"Ironic."

"My luck is just that good," he joked, mimicking my earlier phrasing.

"You're super late. Did you get a note from office?"

"Nope. New kid, remember? I think that's part of initiation too." He smirked and turned to walk down the east hall. "You're the first person that has talked to me today, Avery Brave. So, thanks for that. I'll see ya around."

"Good luck," I said casually and gave him a half wave as we parted ways in the hall.

I fought against the smile that crept along my lips and cheeks all the way to class. If I embraced the smile, I may have had to admit to Mother later that her prayers may have been answered. I may have made a new friend.

2.

Perfect, I thought as I slid in behind a computer in the back row. *The entire football team is in my keyboarding class.*

"Avery?" the teacher said, drawing all the attention to me as I tried to slip in incognito.

"Yes?"

"Do you have a reason for being so late to class?"

"Yes, Mrs. Castlebeck. I have a note here from the office."

"First day of school and already in the office, eh, Avery?" said a taunting voice from the opposite side of the room. A voice that sent smoke out of my nostrils and a shiver up my spine. *Ace Wentworth.* I shot a glare at him as I walked my note to the front of the room. He'd ruined last year for me, but this year, I would go down swinging.

"Ace. Did I ask you to assist in this?" the teacher retorted, which gave me great pleasure, and I let my face express it without even trying to mask it.

Ace grumbled a no and glared back at me as I returned to my seat. I caught the amused eyes of several other players on my way back to my seat. Bo Dirk, Sam Hassel, and Nate Reinhart all smirked at me while their cheerleader counterparts giggled and whispered to them.

I had finished the last six months of school at home last year because of all the drama that had ensued following my breakup with Ace, and all his teammate friends knew it. In fact, the whole school knew it.

I finished my typing assignment quickly and proceeded to write Carol a long diatribe about the morning so far. I included a eulogy for the death of locker #733, which I found highly amusing. Towards the end of the email, I found myself no longer writing but instead bargaining with God, even though I knew better, to give me good things this year to make up for last year and help me make it through. In exchange, I would try to be nice to everyone—despite how they had treated me last year.

"I know this is the first day of school, but we are diving in head first. This Friday night is our first pep rally, and we're going to do something that we haven't done before. We're going to write a piece on the pep rally and the game from two different perspectives. One team member, one student body member."

I perked up. I'd already been thinking about my angle for the pep rally piece, so I had zoned out while Mr. Knight was going through the syllabus. *A team member is joining me on this piece? Great.*

"Nate Reinhart, the running back, has agreed to help Avery Brave write the article."

Nate Reinhart? I thought grimly. *Why would he agree to do this? More like forced, probably by the coach.* I imagined threats of getting benched if he didn't help the newspaper—or the other alternative; he could be getting extra credit for doing it. Either way, I resented it. I had to do a group project with one of Ace's best friends. *This is not really what I had in mind, God.*

"Avery Brave, you'll need to get with Nate to secure his notes and help work the two sections together into one piece. We want something that contrasts the perspectives but flows cohesively. Are you good with that?"

"Yes, Mr. Knight," I said dutifully. "May I ask a question, though?"

"Sure."

"What are we trying to accomplish with having the two viewpoints. Isn't it enough to have a non-biased reporter cover the event?"

"Well, I have a hard time believing that you, Avery Brave, are non-biased." He laughed, and I shrugged. "But aside from that, there are two sides to every story, and we are going to be focusing this year on how to tell both sides. Sometimes, it's in an interview; sometimes, it's in working with another reporter or writer; and sometimes, it's about simply trying to see things from someone else's point of view. Fair enough?"

I begrudgingly nodded. "Fair enough."

This was not one of the things that was going to help me be nicer to certain people. *I knew bargaining with God wouldn't work so well,* I chided myself, knowing that I was being childish.

As I hitched my backpack on my shoulder, I was surprised to find Felix still at school; I was there after hours. "Did you survive your first day?" I asked chummily. "What are you still doing here? Get detention on the first day?"

He looked up from his phone as he slouched on a bench outside the front of the school. "Oh, hey. Yeah, I guess I survived. I'm alive." He stood up from the bench, and I was reminded how tall and looming he was. His large brown eyes smiled. "And no to the detention comment."

"And yet you seem to have lost some pep," I observed as I sat down next to him. "First days are the worst. At least for people like me."

"I don't disagree. But how do you mean?"

"All the rest of these people have been hanging out all summer. They all travel in packs. I don't really. I don't fit the All Saints mold. My folks just want me to go here."

Felix nodded and smirked at me. "I think we'll get along just fine. And, for the record, pep is the worst. I doubt I lost any."

I couldn't tell if he was being flirtatious or just funny. I trusted my gut that it was the latter.

"You need a ride or anything? Not that I have a car yet, but my Dad is going to pick me up, and we can drop you somewhere."

"I was going to ask you the same thing."

"I'm confused." I looked at him quizzically.

"I thought you might need a ride."

"You waited for me?"

"Maybe." He shrugged nonchalantly.

"But I was in Newspaper. You waited? Just to see if I needed a ride?"

"Yes. I thought we already established that," he said dryly.

"We did. I'm just shocked."

"Why? Just thought the new kids should stick together."

"We just met, like, a minute ago. The only other person I know who would wait on me was Carol."

"Who's Carol?"

"My best friend. She moved last year."

"Well, see? Then you need someone else to wait on you and give you a ride."

"It's good logic, to be sure, but nonetheless surprising from someone on his first day at All Saints Academy. And maybe a little creepy. I don't even know you," I said facetiously.

"I'm full of surprises. Come on. Let's get coffee on the way to your house."

"K. Let me check in with my Dad."

I watched him walk toward his truck as the call rang on the other end.

"How's my girl?" My Dad's hearty voice rang in my ear,

causing a smile to hook at the corner of my mouth as I said hello.

"I made a new friend today, and he's offered me a ride home. Just wanted to make sure that was okay."

He paused before asking, "You feel okay about it?"

"Yes, sir. He's new here. I'm sort of new here. So, I think we might be good friends. He seems like a good guy."

"Alright. How long does it take to get to the house? You have your mace?"

"Eight minutes flat. Ten with traffic. And yes. Left pocket in my pack."

"Alright, text me when you get home. I'll expect it in ten minutes."

I smiled. "Thanks, Dad."

"You bet, Avery Brave. Proud of you."

"You're proud of me for getting a ride home from a boy I just met? This seems backward, Mr. Nightingale."

His laugh was just as hearty as his voice as he said, "It's much bigger than that, and you know it."

"Yes, sir. I'll text you soon."

3.

"How was the first day, dear?" Mother asked as she passed the potatoes across to my father.

"It had its highs and its lows," I said as I moved the tomatoes in my salad around my plate.

"Which should we start with?" my father inquired, winking at me, fully aware of what I should lead with.

"Why don't you start with who brought you home? Your father said a friend brought you home?" she asked without masking her concern.

I smiled, thinking back to my interactions with Felix that day. "I'd say he's part of the high. I made a new friend today. His name is Felix, and he's the new kid at Saints this year."

"Oh, it's a boy?" Mother clarified not-so-subtly.

"Yes, Mom, but he's just a friend. Promise," I assured her, reaching over to pat her arm. "But I made a friend, just like you prayed," I said, hoping to distract her from the boy subject.

"But just to clarify, he is a boy?" she continued.

"Dinah, relax," my father coddled with a sip of his tea. "Where is he transferring from?" he asked me.

"His father is in the military, and they just moved here."

"Ah, I see. I bet he's moved around a lot. That was good of you to befriend him on his first day, Avery. Well done."

"Well, that's the funny part," I said. "I was the only one that spoke to him this morning, but I feel like, mostly, he befriended me. He even waited for me after the newspaper to see if I needed a ride home."

Mother's eyebrows went to the top of her forehead while she folded her mashed potatoes with her meatloaf.

"And you're sure he's just a friend, dear?"

"Yeah, mom. Just friends."

"Moving on, Dinah…," Dad said, coming to my aid.

"Ok, Clive, you're right," she finally relented.

Dad nodded and smiled at her. "So what was the low?"

I sighed at the memory. "I have to do this story for the paper on the pep rally Friday night, and they assigned a football player to essentially co-write it with me."

"It's not Ace, is it?" my Father's brows practically soared with concern.

"No, to my relief, it's not. I think I would have quit the paper if that had happened."

"Now, Avery…," Mother started in but then paused. "Never mind. That's fair."

"So, who is it?" Dad continued.

"Nate Reinhart."

"Isn't he the running back?" Dad seemed more interested than concerned now.

"I think so…," I answered, keeping my tone aloof.

"So, why don't you want to write it with him?"

"I just don't *love* football players," I admitted as I swirled my potatoes in a clockwise pattern. Mom reached across the table and patted my arm.

"Avery Brave, I understand where you're coming from—believe me, I do—but they aren't all the same."

"But they are all kind of friends. Today, Ace mocked me in class, and they all sort of joined in—like they have inside jokes about Avery Brave," I said, using air quotes in irritation, "which I'm sure they actually do, come to think of it."

Dad put his fork down and looked at me seriously but thoughtfully. "So maybe the low is more that Ace is still able to be in school? And maybe that we wanted you to not run away from him?"

I sighed heavily and shrugged my shoulders. They felt like they weighed fifty pounds each. Dad was right. The weight of Ace Wentworth was going to follow me around school all year. Maybe longer.

"Probably," I said solemnly. "Plus, I don't have Carol."

Mom and Dad exchanged a sympathetic look.

"I know it's hard," Mom empathized, "But maybe this Felix guy will turn out to be a good friend."

"I could see that." I was surprised that she had dropped her judgment of the idea of a male friend.

"As long as he's just a friend?" she added just in time.

"Yes, Mother," I said with a quiet smirk. "He's funny and flirtatious, but not in a way that makes me think he wants to date me or anything."

"Want to invite him to sit with us at the game?"

"Sure, I guess." Feeling suddenly uninterested in anything since the conversation had taken a decidedly Ace turn, I found it hard to recover.

"Would ice cream cheer you up?" Mom said in a perky voice, whisking our plates from the table.

"Always," I said flatly, smiling at Dad, who winked at me.

"Any new teachers this year?" Mom asked from the kitchen.

"Not that I know of. Everyone returned."

"That's rare, huh?"

"I know, right? Usually, we Saints are pretty good at running people off."

Dad laughed, and Mother tried not to in order let me know she didn't approve of my snarkiness or poking fun at saints.

"Enough about me, though. How was y'all's day?"

We talked about Dad's client merger and Mom's book club and new plants she bought at a fundraiser while we ate Rocky Road ice cream—my dad's favorite, though I prefer mint chip.

After dessert, I excused myself and got ready for bed, waiting on the time zones to align perfectly for me to be able to Facetime with Carol. I was excited to tell her about Felix.

Before I headed up the stairs, Mom caught up to me.

"I want to apologize about this morning," she said. "I realized later that I was anxious about you going back. I'm sorry I was so negative. You looked wonderful. You are wonderful. You're our brave girl—for many reasons. Okay?"

I smiled, feeling a bit better. "Thanks, Mom."

The next day at school, I saw Felix in our "dark corner," as he now called it because the last panel of fluorescent lights had already gone out. He gave me his phone number and told me to text him if I wanted to eat outside with him at lunch. I told him I did, but I had to find a way to talk to Nate without getting barraged by the whole team.

Felix laughed. "Good luck with that."

As it turned out, though, I could eat outside, because, in keyboarding, Nate sent me a message and told me to meet him in the gym after school so we could talk about the article. I didn't like the idea of being alone with him in the gym after school, but I figured the cheerleaders were having practice, which is why he'd chosen that location, so I said it was fine. At lunch, I told Felix about meeting Nate after school, and he asked if he should wait on me again.

"Are you sure?" I asked, not wanting to abuse his driving status.

"Yeah. My parents aren't home till later—plus, from your descriptions, yours seem nicer anyway." He winked.

"Oh! That reminds me: my mom wanted me to tell you that you're welcome to sit with us during the game if you want on Friday."

He raised his eyebrows in mock-alarm. "I'm shocked, Avery Brave! You don't sit in the student section?"

"You're probably *not* shocked, and I don't peg you for someone who would sit there either," I jousted back.

"Too true. Correctly pegged. My parents will be out of town that night anyway. Sounds fun."

"Cool." I nodded as the bell rang. "Well, see you after school then."

"See ya."

Mr. Knight stopped by my desk after the bell rang as I was loading my bag.

"This isn't really my business, but I heard some other girls talking about how they 'couldn't believe you would even consider working with Nate after last year'." He mimicked them gently in a pretend girlish voice. "I know Nate and Ace are friends, right? So, I just wanted to make sure this was all above board, and you were okay."

My stomach sank a bit at being the subject of gossip, but I rallied for Mr. Knight. "I appreciate the concern, Mr. Knight. I appreciate the mockery even more. It's not my favorite, but I can make it work."

He nodded and let me pass towards the door.

"Don't take crap from anybody, Miss Nightingale," he said as a last-minute caution that I knew was more than what he was saying.

"I'll give hell if they try, sir." I nodded and gave a slight wave. "See ya tomorrow."

He waved back, and I walked out and headed toward the gym.

Nate was leaning against the back wall on the top bleacher in the basketball gym playing a game on his phone while the cheerleaders tried to impress him below on the court. Nate was one of the most sought-after boys in our school, and it was clear that several of the cheerleaders were trying to get his attention. But it was also obvious he didn't care that they were there; I had misjudged that part. Maybe he hadn't chosen this location because of them. I took a deep breath and decided to try and be nice. Maybe it was just a central location.

"Hey," I said, sitting down fairly far away from him. Even from a distance, I could tell how tall he was, towering above me even sitting down. Then again, I was only 5'3", so everyone seemed to tower over me.

Pulling out a notebook, my phone, and a pen, I set my backpack to the side. I was ready to get this over with, but he was still playing on his phone.

Be nice, I reminded myself. "So, do you want to just get me some notes on Saturday or Sunday, and I can piece the article together?"

He looked up from his phone. His deep blue eyes conveyed shock. "You don't want to actually write it together?"

"Oh!" I said, almost dropping my pencil. "I just assumed you got roped into doing this and didn't really have any interest in writing it with me." Now, I was the one who was befuddled.

"No," was all he said as he looked back to his phone.

I was so confused. *This is going nowhere.* Knowing what I knew about football and football players, if the team lost, Nate might not actually feel like writing this at all on Saturday or Sunday.

"Why don't you just let me know on Saturday what you want to do? You can send me notes, or we can meet somewhere," I said, offering a solution.

"Fine. Whatever," he said, not looking up from his phone.

I took out a piece of paper and laid it on the bleacher between us. "Here are some leading questions that may help you take mental or actual notes that will help us write the article."

Nate's jaw tightened, and he shot me a glare. "I know how to write a paper, Avery."

As he said my name, it had such bite to it, and I hated the way it sounded coming off his tongue. I'd managed to insult him the very first time I had ever talked to him this year. *Bravo, Avery Brave.* This being nice thing was harder than I'd thought.

"I'm sorry. I didn't mean for it…I was just trying to be helpful," I said, stuffing my notebook back in my bag as quickly as I could.

"Whatever. I'll call you on Saturday." The irritation was clear in his voice.

I stood to leave. Then, realizing a problem, I turned back to him. "But you don't have my number."

Looking at me sideways, he raised his eyebrows and fired a

low blow. "Yea...but Ace does."

I seethed. *Oh! You're going to bring him into this? That's it, I'm done being nice.* I glared at him and let the gym door slam behind me. The heavy door boomed and echoed throughout the now-empty school. I felt satisfied even though a door slamming did not teach Nate a lesson in any way.

I stormed all the way to the front of the building, where I knew Felix would be waiting, thinking of fiery comebacks I should have, could have said to put Nate Reinhart in his place.

Then, I stopped, dropping my backpack on the floor and pacing back and forth, feeling angry. *Why did he even have to bring him up?! Did he agree to do this article just to mess with me? How am I supposed to do this, God?* I half-thought, half-prayed forcefully with my hands on my temples. *Sabotage.*

I finally picked up my bag again, feeling calmer, and headed toward the front doors. I slowed as I walked by the front office. The semi-circle had open offices in the front and closed offices in the back for Principal Sands and the assistant principal, Mr. Hickham. While their offices had doors, the back walls that faced the western hallway were entirely made of glass. The panes looked like blocks of ice so that you couldn't really see in, but it gave both parties the illusion of transparency.

All the lights were off except a desk lamp. There were two people in Mr. Hickham's office, though I couldn't see who. One was taller, and one was about my height but slightly taller. Either they were talking very closely or they were kissing.

No one should be kissing in the school after hours! Or during *hours, for that matter. That sort of behavior is not allowed on campus. That's more public school behavior,* I joked to myself. And it was in Mr. Hickham's office! *So...,* I thought, *who could be kissing in there?? Maybe his wife stopped by? I don't think he's married. Maybe it's just some kids messing around and pulling pranks?*

As I was trying to concoct a scenario in which I could waltz in, pretending to have a question to ask, and catch them in the act, I heard a hushed and seductive voice. "Mr. Hickham..."

I didn't need to hear the rest. The tone of her voice and the way she said "Mr." told me all I needed. *It was a student!* I ran out the front doors and practically knocked Felix to the ground where he was posted up on one of the entrance pillars. He steadied himself and caught me by the shoulders.

"Are you okay?" he asked, as if I was crazy. "Are you running away from Nate?" he laughed.

"No. I mean, at first, I was storming out, yes. But then...." I caught my breath. "I just saw something in Mr. Hickham's office!"

Felix's eyes lit up. "Pray tell, Nancy Drew!" he mocked with a face full of fake excitement.

"Stop. I'm being serious. At first, I couldn't tell who was in there. But then I heard a girl say, 'Mr. Hickham'...."

"A girl?"

"I was running back from the gym when I slowed by Mr. Hickham's office." I paused, starting to pace in little steps, each time turning in my heel. "It looked through the glass like someone was embracing, kissing even. Then, I heard a voice say, 'Mr. Hickham'." I imitated the sultry way she had said the name.

"Ew. Don't do that," he joked.

"Her voice sounded like mine. It wasn't an adult. It was definitely a girl. A student, maybe."

"A student is in there with Mr. Hickham?! In a school - business kind of way or...something else?"

"I just did the voice, didn't I? Yes. In a comprisatory way. "

Felix blinked. "I don't think you did that right."

"Did what?" I said, feeling a little disoriented.

"I think you mean 'compromising way.' But listen, you can't just go around accusing people of stuff like that. You have to be sure."

"I know. And I'm *not* sure. I sort of panicked and ran out," I said, imitating and flapping my arms nervously.

"And now, I'm up to speed."

"Yep."

"Wow. What a turn of events, eh?"

"I know. What should we do? Should I go back in there?" I bit my nails, starting back toward the door, feeling both excited from the rush of adrenaline and scared at having witnessed, however indirect, a crime.

"First, you need to calm down, because you're acting like a squirrel," Felix said, grabbing me by the shoulders to stop me from going back in.

"Sorry. I get excited. And I feel...like I need to figure this out. If this is at all what I think it is, I have to figure it out."

"Hence the Nancy Drew comment."

"I resent that, by the way," I retorted.

"You resent it or you resemble it?" He gave me a snarky look, then moved on. "Second, we need to keep this to ourselves until we have more clues. Okay?"

"Right."

"Did Nate see?'

"No. He was so impossible! I left him in the gym. I could have slapped him."

"What did he say?"

As we got in Felix's car, I explained. "It might surprise you to know, but I dated Ace Wentworth last year." I paused to let him respond, but he didn't. "And Nate took the opportunity to rub that in. I said he didn't have my number, and he said he could get it from Ace." My eyes narrowed at the memory.

Felix still didn't respond. He continued to look thoughtfully out the front windshield, which made me think that I had overreacted to what Nate had said. After a few moments passed and I could stand his lack of response no longer, I asked him if he was okay.

"Sorry," he said, finally looking at me. "I guess I got lost in trying to think of what to say. It's just that I've already heard the stories," he admitted as he pulled up to my house. "I hate that I have. We're just becoming friends."

I groaned as I opened the door. "I hate this school. You've only been here, what, all of two days and someone already told you the story?" I growled as I slammed the door behind me for the second time today. I knew it wasn't Felix I was mad at. I heard him scramble out of the car and come after me and felt the heat of embarrassment crawl up my neck.

"Avery—wait," he called.

I dropped my bag and crossed my arms. "What?"

"It's just that the stories bother me. I know they are not the whole story, and I know we don't know each other well enough yet to divulge all our secrets yet. But I still don't like it. I didn't know what to say."

I nodded awkwardly as the door opened and Mother popped her head out. "Everything alright out here? Oh!" she said, wiping her hands on her apron. "Hello—you must be Felix."

Felix stuck his hand out to shake hers without missing a beat. "Nice to meet you, Mrs. Nightingale."

"Is everything alright, Avery?"

I nodded and walked past her inside. "Yes. The wake of Ace Wentworth is mighty wide," I mumbled.

Mother made face at Felix and said, "Ah, yes. Would you like to stay for dinner, Felix?"

"No, thank you, ma'am. I should be getting home. But thank you, Mrs. Nightingale. Avery," he called past my mother, "I'll call you later, okay?"

I nodded as I walked to the kitchen. I could hear Mother tell him that it was nice to meet him.

"Well, thank you for inviting me to the game. I'll see you then."

"Oh, good, then you'll sit with us?"

"Yes, ma'am."

"Wonderful. See you then, Felix."

After that, I heard the door shut and his car drive away. I hadn't been very nice to Nate or to Felix today. I knew they were just victims who happened to be in the way. The object of my fury was really Ace.

Over a plate of apples and peanut butter dip, I told Mom everything that had happened that day. Venting about it helped enough that I calmed down and stopped trying to envision Ace in an alley, dead, or in jail. I helped Mother make dinner and set the table but then excused myself to go call Carol before it was time for dinner.

"Are you sure Felix isn't trying to date you?" Carol asked after I told her about my day.

"No, I promise. There's nothing there."

"Nothing? No tension? No staring when he thinks you're not looking? No longing in his eyes?"

"That's enough, Dr. Carol—no more love analysis. But for the record, really, no. He feels like a brother or something. He's funny and considerate, and he's extremely good looking, don't get me wrong, but there's nothing there."

"So…you did notice!"

"Carol, stop."

"Sorry. What about Nate?"

"What about him?"

"What's he like? Besides gorgeous."

"Yeah, but he's such a jerk that it really takes away from the beautiful factor."

"Impossible. Plus, all the model-worthy ones are jerks."

"That's terrible, Carol. I don't want to believe that. There have to boys that exist that are both honorable and pretty," I joked.

"Yeah, maybe in Utopia."

"Or heaven." We both giggled. It was good to talk and laugh with Carol. It was almost as good as having her there with me.

"So, what's it like wearing real clothes to school?" I teased as the conversation turned to lighter subjects like public school, music, and the movies that were coming out that we both wanted to see. We talked until Mother called me down for dinner.

At the table, I retold all of the day's events to my Dad, and, by the end of the night, I felt better. I knew I needed to call Felix and apologize.

"Hey," I said sheepishly as he answered the phone.

"Hey."

"I'm sorry about earlier."

"Don't be. I'm sorry. I hate that people tell stories that aren't theirs to tell. I'm sorry about what happened with Ace, and you can tell me your side whenever you feel like it. Sorry you have to deal with Nate, too. If I need to show him some army combat moves, I can."

"Thanks. I think I'll be fine. And I'm sorry for storming off. It wasn't you. Okay? We're okay?" I asked.

"Yep." I could hear the smile in his voice.

"See you tomorrow," I said.

"See you in our dark corner."

4.

The gym was hot and sticky, though every door and window was open. The drums rattled my ribs and echoed in my chest. The band swayed and bounced and made the whole left side of the stands seem like it was moving. Pom-poms rustled and shimmered as the lights went down except for a spotlight, shining on a precisely formed huddle of girls.

The music swelled as I took my seat on the third bench from the front and slipped my media badge over my head. The hip hop beat was loud and a bit too seductive, I thought, but the bass rumbled in my bones, and I had to admit their movements were tight and on point.

I never really understood the point of dancers at sporting events. Lately, it was more of a mild distraction during halftime, but it was clearly over-sexualized, especially for a private Christian school. This come-hither cheer was solely for the football players and not at all for the pep of the school as a whole—not that I would put that in the article, though.

Of course, I supposed maybe it rallied the crowd anyway. The students and parents went wild as the cheerleaders ran off the gym floor. I sighed heavily in the midst of the clapping and screaming so no one would hear me. *This is the worst.*

The drumline made their way onto the floor and formed a tight row. Their beats collided, diverted in choreographed directions and tempos, and blended back together in a wild crescendo before dropping out. I actually clapped and cheered—I love drums, and they were really good.

Principle Sands and Assistant Principle Hickham walked out to the center of the floor. I couldn't help but think about who had been in the office with Mr. Hickham.

"Alright, settle down, Saints," Mr. Sands said into the mic. A lull rippled through the crowd, but no one sat. "Without further ado, please give it up for your starting lineup Saints!"

I counted fifteen boys as they ran out of the locker room onto the floor through a cloud of fog. They all pumped their fists and signaled for the crowd to get louder and rowdy. One boy even took his shirt off and swung it above his head. I saw several teachers rolling their eyes and shaking their heads.

Among the starters were the boys from my keyboarding class. I caught Nate's eye for a split second, but I looked away, sliding behind a tall boy in front of me in hopes that neither he nor Ace could spot me.

I cringed as I heard Ace's voice echo in the microphone. "We are the Saints, and we won't take no for answer!"

The crowd went wild.

"We are the Saints, and we take victory for ourselves!"

This crowd is going insane over a speech that lacks any real motivation and, frankly, has terrible theology, I argued to myself.

"We are the Saints, and we cannot lose!"

At that, the crowd really lost it.

But that's not actually true, I thought. Then again, Ace usually didn't see how wrong he was.

Everyone was jumping around like it was a trampoline convention and sweating wildly, shouting out the words that Ace had just motivated them with. They had hung on every syllable.

They finally softened to a throbbing roar when head coach Hayden walked out. Head coach Hayden Butler was a favorite among the girls for his scruffy facial hair and wavy brown locks that flipped out at the base of his hat. Personally, I thought Mr. Knight was more attractive. *But that's not the point*, I reminded myself.

Coach Hayden told everyone to calm down. "I'm really proud of these guys out here." He put an arm on Nate's shoulder. "They have been working hard, and we are going to leave it all out on the field tonight. Nate is going to lead us in prayer."

My eyebrows would not come down from my hairline as I bowed my head and closed my eyes. Nate? Why? But his voice was velvety and strong as he asked God's protection as they played and asked God's favor for the outcome. It was short but clear.

Everyone said amen, and the players walked off as the cheerleaders and the band filled the court. After our alma mater and the fight song, the rally was finally over.

I hung around near the court as students celebrated all the

pep and their apparent inevitable victory, according to Ace. I got a quote from a cheerleader and a band member. Suddenly, Coach Hayden was standing alone, no longer in serious playmaking conversations or bombarded by hyper players. I dashed over to him.

"Coach, I'm Avery Brave with the All Saints Bugle."

"I know you who you are, Ms. Nightingale." He smiled.

"Oh. Okay. Well, I wondered if I could get a statement for the article Nate and I are writing together?"

"Sure thing."

We talked for a moment, and I scribbled down his words, but just behind the coach in my line of sight was Nate, walking toward us. Was he coming over here? After the way he acted yesterday? The audacity.

Just then, Ace stepped in front of him, blocking his path and keeping him from getting any closer—purely for intimidation, I surmised.

I thanked the coach and slipped out the side door before Ace or Nate could notice.

"What have I missed?" Felix said, sitting down beside me with the largest soda I'd ever seen.

"Caffeine much?" I teased.

"Don't judge." He pretended to glare at me. "Now, what have I missed?"

My father leaned forward and shook Felix's hand across me and answered, "First half. We're up by two, first down."

"Thanks, sir. Nice to see you."

I smiled at Felix and shook my head slightly. He shrugged and whispered low, "What is so amusing, Avery Brave?"

"You're soooo polite."

He laughed. "Military father, remember?"

I made small "o" with my mouth and looked back to the game just in time to see Nate catch the toss, tucking it in tight against his ribs and making a move toward the end zone. I knew I didn't know that much about football, but, while Felix pointed out which player was in what position, I could see what was coming a mile away, and it all seemed to be happening in slow motion. The outside linebacker approached aggressively, causing Nate to turn back toward the other defenders. The defensive end aimed low and hit him right in the knees...hard. Nate started to flip forward just in time for the perfectly placed linebacker to aim high, hitting him helmet to helmet. I couldn't be sure if it was linebacker impact or when his helmet whiplashed against the ground, but there was no mistaking that, when the play was over, Nate was out cold.

Everyone gasped and stood to their feet.

Nate lay unmoving on the ground.

The referee blasted the whistle and charged, along with the coaches, over to Nate. The referee threw the defensive back and the linebacker off the field. Everyone hovered over Nate for minutes. A woman who I could only guess was Nate's mother ran to the fence, hysterical.

Suddenly, the night was still except for the ambulance sirens starting to wail and grow nearer. The stadium lights suddenly seemed like spotlights on Nate's still body lying on the turf.

The trainers and medics kneeled next to him, taking his helmet off and trying to assess his body. The whole team respectfully took a knee and waited pensively. Felix nudged me with his elbow, and I shrugged at him, not knowing what to say or do. My Mother leaned across my Father and whispered, "Is that the boy that you're writing with?" I nodded, and she said, "Gracious."

Several "he's not getting ups" rippled through the crowd, and a second gasp erupted as the medics walked a stretcher out onto the field. Nate's girlfriend/cheerleader counterpart, Sylvie, seemed unaffected, huddled together with the other cheerleaders, whispering. Her face was not distraught or concerned in any way, which I noted as odd and cold. Felix appeared to notice it too.

As they carried Nate off the field with his mom and dad running close behind to get in the ambulance, the referee began arguing with the opposing team's coach, the coach yelling and pointing fingers until the referee signaled that the coach was ejected as well. All three—the defensive end, the linebacker, and the coach—ranted all the way off the field.

Mother shook her head and said, "Disgraceful. Two Christian schools, and they can't even act like it on the field. And it's only the second quarter."

Felix and I laughed to ourselves and exchanged glances

where she couldn't see. While the game continued, I found myself more concerned about Nate than I was about the score. But I forced myself to focus on the game in order to write the article effectively—now, for the both of us.

Two days later, sitting in church, I still couldn't get Nate off my mind. The empty seats where his whole family usually sat were a constant reminder of him. *Should I go check on him? Should I even ask about the article? Is he in a coma? Why can't I stop thinking about him?*

We sang three more songs, and the service ended. I thought about going over to some of his church friends to ask how he was, but I didn't. Instead, as I joined the crowd heading up the aisle, I found myself wondering if Felix and his parents went to church. They had never visited our church that I knew of, and he had never mentioned it. Not that it really mattered—half the kids at our school went to our church but acted like anything but a saint or a Christian.

Dad always said there was a church and a bank on every corner in the south with fast food in between. It was certainly true in our city. Dad would also always tell us stories of the small town that he grew up in, and, while it sounded nice to know everyone, it also sounded suffocating.

Over lunch, mom asked about the article and questioned me on how I was going to get it done. I told her I didn't know, because I didn't know how Nate was.

"I actually heard from Mrs. Reinhart that he had a concussion and a broken ankle. But he's not in a coma like some of the kids were saying."

I looked at her sideways. "How do you know that? And since when do you talk to Mrs. Reinhart?"

"Avery! Watch you tone, please," my dad reprimanded me.

"Sorry, I was just surprised. It came out edgier than it sounded in my head."

"Mrs. Reinhart is in my book club, Avery Brave, and I called her to check on Nate yesterday," Mom said while she served me more salad. "He's at home now. I think you should go check on him, and then you could talk about the article."

"At his house?"

"Sure. Why not," Mom insisted.

"It just doesn't seem like a very neutral place, that's all."

"Why do you need neutrality?" Dad chimed in. "Not that I'm protesting the concept or the wisdom, just curious."

"We just…don't really get along."

"Oh," Mom said. "Have you tried to be nice?"

"Yes, Mom," I said, annoyed. "Why do you always assume it's on my end that things are failing?"

"She has a point, Dinah. Getting along is a quid pro quo thing," Dad aided again.

"Are you sure?" Mother asked again.

"*Yes*, Mom. I told you what he said! I'm shocked you would be encouraging this, considering…"

"Well, maybe you should take him a get-well balloon and try a little harder to be nice. He has been through an ordeal. And, after all, the article will most likely be about him now.…"

"I am not taking him a balloon." I shook my head.

"Don't take him a balloon," my dad echoed.

"No?" Mom asked, almost defending her suggestion.

"No," my dad said flatly. "You don't take a boy balloons. Unless he's five."

"Ok, I just thought it would be a nice gesture."

"I think me going over that there at all is gesture enough."

"Truth," my dad said, finishing his steak and putting his fork down. I smiled at him, and he winked at me.

"Okay…," Mom conceded as she cleared the table.

"I need to go see a client this afternoon, so I can drop you by if you want," Dad offered.

"Okay," I said grudgingly.

Dad dropped me off and told me he'd be back within twenty minutes. I walked up the grand stone staircase to the front door. I knocked three times on the ornate door and waited, half-expecting a butler to answer. I heard an "I got it" yelled behind the door just before Nate's little brother, Tanner, opened it.

"Hey. Avery, isn't it?"

Tanner was shorter than Nate was but still much taller than me. He was a freshman this year and already seemed to be quite popular.

"Yes, it's Avery Brave."

"Come on in. He's up in his room."

I looked around the foyer, which looked more like a hotel than a house. "Um…," I began, "I don't know where that is."

Tanner was halfway in the other room when he turned. "Oh! Sorry, I assumed you guys were friends. He talks about you sometimes. My bad. I'll show you."

"No. We're not friends," I protested, probably too much. *He talks about me? Great, he probably makes fun of me to his family, too,* I thought bitterly. "Could you just tell him I'm here to work on our project? Maybe he's not up for it." I suddenly realized I hadn't thought this through enough. *I wish he was laid up on the couch. Maybe he'll refuse to see me, and I can leave.*

"Oh, you're here to work on a project? I doubt you'll get much out of him." Tanner laughed. "He's hopped up on pain killers. And he's laid up in bed; he can't really come down."

"Oh," I said, following Tanner up the stairs. *Great, just great.*

Tanner knocked on the door and waited for an answer before he stuck his head in the door, "You decent?"

Nate simply grunted from across the room.

"Avery is here. To see you," he added at the last second. I attempted to open my mouth to object, but nothing came out.

"Oh," was all Nate said. Tanner told me that he'd just taken another dose and wouldn't last long and then disappeared down the hall, leaving me standing in the doorway to Nate Reinhart's bedroom.

He was propped up on at least four pillows with another three under his casted ankle. His room was pale gray with navy bedspread and navy curtains. There were framed and signed jerseys on the walls alongside movie posters. His head fell to the side, and he looked at me as if he was drunk. "You coming or going?"

I sighed. This was worse than talking to mean Nate. "Coming, I guess."

He patted the bed next to him. "Have a seat, then."

I am not sitting on the bed next to him, I thought. But, looking around the room, I saw there was nowhere else to sit except for his game chair, which looked more like a crescent moon than a chair. I picked the farthest corner of the bed and sat down gingerly.

"So, you've come to check on me?" he said as his eyes drooped closed.

"No," I corrected, "I came to—uh—" I corrected myself, "I came to tell you not to worry about the article. Obviously, I can write it myself."

"I have notes, though…about at least the rally." His eyes opened again, and he reached a hand towards me as the words jumbled. He squinted his eyes. I did not reach back. "I'm about the other day sorry." He slurred the mixed-up words as they came out.

I smirked. He was out of his mind. No doubt he wouldn't remember any of this later. "You're sorry?"

"I was a jerk of all jerks to you." He paused, finally dropping his outstretched hand. "But I usually am, aren't I?"

Well, at least he's honest when he's out of his mind.

"Wasn't I?" he insisted.

I nodded.

He clutched his chest. "Oh, Avery Brave!"

I looked around the room in embarrassment, expecting a camera crew to jump out and tell me I was being punked. *This is just the painkillers*, I reminded myself.

"Please! Please-please-please forgive me."

"Okay, okay—be quiet. I forgive you," I hushed him, completely uncomfortable and embarrassed.

"Avery—come here." He patted the bed beside him.

"No," I said.

"Avery, come here. I need to tell you something."

"No. I'm not coming over there. You can tell me from here."

"I was a jerk because…Sylvie broke—I broke up…we broke up."

No wonder she didn't seem concerned at the game.

"I told you to meet me there because I wanted her to piss-off," he said, slurring the last part.

"I think you mean…never mind." I stopped. There was no point in correcting him.

"But then, she wasn't even at practice. I thought it would make her jealous, but she didn't even see."

"It's fine. I'm sorry you guys broke up."

"No!" he practically shouted. "I'm sorry. I'm sorry for what I said about Ace."

"It's fine. I don't want to talk about Ace."

Nate held up his hands in surrender. "I don't want to talk about him either. I want to talk about you."

But before he could say anything more, I blurted, "You said you had notes for me? I can just write the article."

"Over there," he slurred, closing his eyes again as he pointed to his backpack on the hook on the wall. He started snoring, and I sighed, realizing I was going to have to go through it myself to find the notes. But at least he forgot about talking about me.

I unzipped the biggest zipper only to find a black folder with my name on it right in the front of the pocket. I opened it to find detailed notes of the rally and thoughts he had written down ahead of time about the game; quotes from the coach, information about the opposing team, and strengths/weakness that our team had against them.

I dawned on me as I retrieved the folder and looked back over at the boy who was propped up and snoring that I may have misjudged him completely. Though I quickly reminded myself of the snide jab he'd made. I couldn't make sense of it.

"Don't look now, but look who's venturing into the dark corner…," Felix whispered as he closed his locker. I looked down the hall to see Nate crutching his way toward us. Felix stood to leave. I grabbed his shirt-tail to try and hold him there, but he escaped me.

"Felix!" I whispered. "Don't you dare."

He turned and flashed me a mischievous grin. "Oh, I do dare," he said and practically jogged away from me down the hallway.

Nate slowly made his way toward me, nodding to Felix as he passed him but looking sheepish as he approached. I thought maybe I could hide behind my locker door, but that was ridiculous, because it only hid my face. Then, I thought I could pretend I didn't see him, but that would be the equivalent of running away from a lame man on the side of the road—cruel and completely unfair. So, I closed my locker and faced him.

"The article was good," he said as he finally reached me, slightly out of breath. I was aware of his woodsy cologne and freshly cut hair that was not as dark as Felix's but a glossy shade of chocolate. I cataloged his dark, impossibly long lashes that blinked over his striking blue eyes. He wasn't as tall as Felix either, but he had an intimidating muscular presence that Felix did not have.

"Thanks," I muttered, trying not to really look at him directly anymore.

"How did you get my notes?"

My mouth fell open, and I practically dropped my English Lit book.

"Um, I got them from your house…?" I reminded him,

wondering if he was being serious. *Does he not remember me being there at all?* It had been almost a week since I had been in his room, and it was the first day I'd seen him at school.

His deep blue eyes widened in horror, and the half-smile he'd had while complimenting the article faded. "You came to my house?"

"You don't remember?"

"No—I—Well, I thought…I assumed," he stammered, "I thought it was the pain killers. I assumed I dreamed it."

Would that be a normal dream? I wondered. *Me at his house? Nothing seems out of place about that even in a dream, Nate? He talked about me to Tanner, and he also dreams about me. No wonder I can't figure this guy out.*

"So, I really said all those things?" He squinted, clearly hoping he hadn't.

"I promise they are already in the vault," I assured him. *Don't tell him there's a vault!* I scolded myself.

He let his head fall back in exasperation and leaned harder on the right crutch, taking the weight off the left ankle and shoulder. "I cannot believe you came to my house to get my notes while I was on pain killers." He sounded more irritated now than embarrassed. *He dreams about me, okay, Avery—he did actually say he dreams about me…but now he's irritated with me?*

"How did you get in? Was my mom there?"

"I don't know. Tanner let me in." I shrugged. "I wasn't there long."

"Of course Tanner let you in. He was loving all the blackmail videos he was getting of me."

"Seriously, Nate nothing happened that's worth talking about." I tried to deflect him, feeling uncomfortable.

"No, I acted like an idiot." He covered his face with his hand. "At one point, didn't I pat the bed and tell you to come over?" He asked, wincing again.

"Nate. It's nothing," I dismissed him, wishing he would just go away so we could both forget. *What does he care anyway?*

"But I did apologize, though, didn't I?"

"I'll take it to my grave. No one has to know," I said, putting him off, hoping he'd let it go.

"Gosh, Avery!" he huffed. I stopped halfway through zipping my backpack and stared at him. He *was* mad. "I came over here to apologize for the other day and try to make it up to you. But you're making it impossible! I wanted to tell you thanks for making the article great even though I couldn't help."

"It wasn't my idea, and I'm just glad it's over," I said, muttering under my breath. He'd come to be nice, and I was the one trying to avoid him. I hated it when Mother was right.

"And I meant that apology. Drugs or no drugs. The other day, I shouldn't have brought Ace into it. It was cruel. You didn't deserve the way I treated you in the gym." He paused, resituating the crutches like he was about to leave. "But you kinda do now."

And he crutched off down the hall. Half of my body wanted to call out after him, maybe even run after him and apologize, but the other half wanted to slam my locker and storm off.

I did the latter.

5.

I doodled in my notebook while I waited on Mr. Knight to arrive in the newspaper room. I thought back to the day that I had stormed out on Nate in the gym and possibly witnessed something in the front office. I wrote down the words MR. HICKHAM and STUDENT followed by a question mark. I wrote down the question WHO WOULD KNOW? Then, I listed everyone who might be a potential lead—cheerleaders, the guidance counselor, and someone on the paper.

Three good places to start, but that would have to wait. Mr. Knight had arrived, setting his messenger bag down on his desk, and was coming over to sit beside me. He'd asked me to meet him after school to talk about a new assignment he was putting me on. I'd never met him after school by myself, much less in his classroom alone, which I knew was against school policy as well as just plain improper (Mother would say), so I asked, "Shouldn't we meet in a more public space, Mr. Knight?"

He laughed through his nose and shook his head. "Avery Brave, I appreciate your tenacity and also your propriety. We won't be alone in a minute. I've asked someone else to join us; they are right outside the door. So, technically, we're not alone. But thank you for caring."

I nodded and looked curiously toward the door, wondering who was outside.

"I wanted to talk to you privately about what I want to do for the rest of this semester."

I was intrigued. Mr. Knight had never given me any assignments that were longer than one article.

"I, as well as most of the other staff, really loved the article that you and Nate wrote this weekend."

"Thank you."

"And, in light of his recent injury, he's most likely out for the rest of the season, so coach and I thought maybe he could write more. Cover a variety of topics. Seeing two different perspectives could be really good for everyone."

I didn't like where this was headed. There was a lump forming in my throat that tasted like selfishness and anger.

"You guys wrote so well together, I'd like to make you a team. A writing team."

Fabulous, I thought, regretting my words to him earlier, wishing I could just forget the whole thing and work alone and hating the way my selfishness tasted.

"Now, you don't really have a choice, because I'm the teacher. But I wanted to have a conversation about it, because you're a good student, and we work really well together on the paper."

And I do appreciate that, really, I do, but come on, Knight! How could you put me with Nate Reinhart for the whole semester?!

"Does he already know? I doubt he'll be thrilled either."

"He does know. He said the same about you. I'm afraid you'll have to work through your differences, history, or whatever is going on and learn to work together—or you'll just funnel that into your writing. Either way, it's up to you." He stood and walked toward the door. "I'm going to let him in now, and we can all talk about how this will work, okay?"

"It's fine. I'm fine, Mr. Knight." I raised my eyebrows, trying to assure him I wasn't angry. Or mostly myself. Either way.

He smiled as if he was proud of me and opened the door. Nate hobbled through the door without looking at me and sat down across from me by Mr. Knight. Mr. Knight explained how he wanted our research, coverage, and writing to go, and we both sat there quietly without looking at each other. I could tell Nate was still mad at me.

This isn't going to work, Lord. You have to get me out of this. I bargained again and begged a little.

There was no answer, and I knew why. God wanted me to learn to be nice, and he was completely okay with this scenario.

Fine. But I don't have to like him. Or trust him.

"Can you both handle that?" I came back in at the end of Mr. Knight's sentence.

I nodded, wondering what it was I was saying I could handle. Nate said, "Fine by me."

"Great. The Back to School dance is this week. That can be your first event to cover together. You'll need to get pictures as well as find a unique angle to report on."

"So, we have to go…together?" I asked, confused. Surely, he didn't mean that we had to go to the dance as a couple.

"You don't have to be each other's date, if that's what you're asking, Avery. But you will need to work together while you're there and write the article together. However that works best is up to you two."

I groaned inside.

Nate crutched out of the classroom, and I gathered my stuff to follow. As I walked out, Mr. Knight said, "Avery, you're fighting this; I can tell. You can't always be the lone ranger, you know."

I nodded. I did know, but I had my reasons, and changing was a whole different thing.

I dodged Nate after that by saying I had to go to the bathroom and hoping he wouldn't wait on me. Since he was clearly mad at me, I didn't think he would.

I didn't have to go to the bathroom, so I just sat in the stall long enough that I thought Nate would leave or Felix would come looking for me. Either one would be okay. I grabbed my bag and was about to open the stall door when several female voices came in the room. I drew my legs up so they couldn't see me from underneath.

The first voice sounded borderline hysterical. "I have to! He said if I didn't come forward that he would."

The second voice was demanding yet feminine. "He wouldn't dare!"

The third voice was slightly mousy but equally as dramatic as the first two. "I think he would. I think he'd dare to do a lot of things. You know what he did to..."

"Don't say it. Don't talk about that!" the second voice interjected.

"But Sylvie, what are you going to do?" said the mousy voice, dialing down the dramatics and getting solemn.

Sylvie? Okay, one voice identified. The first voice was Sylvie. *But who is she talking about?*

"I don't know. This could ruin everything."

"Too true," said the mousy voice, "for both of you."

"Well, don't go near him until you decide. I don't want him bullying you into doing something you can't take back."

"I kinda have to, Whitney. He's my lab partner."

Ok, Whitney is the stern one, Sylvie is the one in trouble, so that makes the mousy one Brooklynn. I'd have to find out who Sylvie's lab partner was. And what they were so concerned about. *And whether there are things a person can actually take back,* I added sarcastically.

"Come on, guys, we're going to be late for practice. And Sylvie already missed too many...because of *him*," Brooklynn said, pushing them out the door.

"I know—and the other day, it went way too far," Sylvie groaned.

"And that's saying something," Brooklynn giggled just before the door squeaked close. Soon, it was quiet again, and I slowly let me legs down and let the blood flow back into them, which caused prickles all the way down. As soon as I could stand, I exited the bathroom slowly, making sure they weren't gathered just beyond the door.

They weren't—but Nate and Felix were. It was strange to see them talking. *Did they have a class together?* They both turned and looked at me at the same time. Felix's eyes smiled, and he laughed. Nate's did not.

"What have you been doing in there? Redecorating?"

"No!" I scolded him with me eyes sarcastically. "I got stuck in a stall while three cheerleaders divulged some cryptic and possibly incriminating secrets."

Nate looked toward the gym, where the girls had walked past them and go in. *Sylvie. Does Nate know anything about this?*

"Really? Pray-tell Nancy!"

I shoved Felix. "Stop calling me Nancy."

"Well! You seem to have a knack for walking into strange situations and finding clues, that's all."

I ignored him and looked cautiously to Nate. "I thought you'd be long gone by now."

"Just needed to talk to you about Friday."

"I'm sorry, I didn't know there was anything to talk about," I said sincerely. "I didn't mean for you to wait on me."

He shot me a glare from under his brows. "I didn't wait on *you*. We need to talk about the assignment." He stood his crutched up and huffed, "Whatever. I'll call you later." And he stormed off the best that someone on crutches can storm. Felix was left wide-eyed in front of me. I shook my head in failure.

"What have you done to the poor invalid?"

"I have no idea." I shrugged and began walking toward the door. "I also seem to have a knack for ticking him off."

"Well, at least tell me all about the cheerleaders in the bathroom."

As we walked to Felix's car, I told him all about what Sylvie, Whitney, and Brooklynn had talked about in the bathroom. As he drove me home, I got out my notebook, where I had doodled earlier about Mr. Hickham, and added the three girls' names and spaces for two possible un-named males.

I wrote the word BLACKMAIL with a questions mark.

I wrote LAB PARTNER, MISSED PRACTICES, and CONTROL. Underneath one of the un-named males, I wrote the phrase PAST

HISTORY. I had more questions than I did answers, but maybe I'd figure it out.

Another thing I needed to figure out was how to work with Nate Reinhart without us killing each other.

"Hey, do you have any classes with Sylvie?"

Felix gave me a suspicious look but said, "Yeah, why?"

"Which class?"

"Biology. Why?"

"Who's her lab partner?"

"It was Nate. But he was just telling me in the hall that the teacher switched him to mine because they broke up. She doesn't know yet. I don't think. Why?"

"Interesting," I said vaguely.

"Would you please tell me what is going on?" Felix demanded, "Your vagueness is very infuriating."

"Well, remember they were telling Sylvie to stay away from him…whoever 'him' is, but she said she can't because he's her lab partner."

"You think they're warning her about Nate?"

"It's just where the clues are leading, that's all." I shrugged. "Maybe she's missed too many practices because of Nate—they were still dating at the time, after all."

As Felix turned in my driveway, he stopped the car and looked at me. "Look I don't know what beef you and Nate have with each other, but I don't think you should jump to conclusions like he's blackmailing Sylvie. I mean, you guys have to work together all semester, so I wouldn't make an enemy of him just yet."

"What do you care?" I huffed and slammed the notebook shut.

"We're friends, aren't we?" His brows lifted, and his eyes conveyed his vulnerability to rejection. I took a deep breath. I certainly didn't want to lose the good thing that was going to get me through this school year.

"We are. I'm sorry." I met his eyes, and mine stung at the thought of crying, which I fought back successfully. "I didn't mean to snap at you, Felix. Please forgive me."

"We're good." He smiled and shifted in his seat to peer at me. "You seem on edge. Want to talk about it?"

"I just seem to be failing epically today. It's gone all wrong. I'm trying to be *nice*, but it's not working. At all."

"I don't know about 'at all,' but, yeah, you've stuck your foot in your mouth more than once. But just like with me, a deep breath and an apology goes a long way. Just wait until Nate calls, and apologize."

"Fine," I muttered reluctantly, knowing he was right but dreading talking to Nate on the phone. "You want to stay for dinner?"

"Thanks, but I should go eat with my folks. Wanna swim after dinner?"

"Yeah, just text me," I said as I got out of his car.

We were still enjoying the heat from the summer—this was the south, after all, and it would be hot well into September. It enabled us to hold on to summer a bit longer even when school started in August. And it had helped me as of late to take my mind off all that was going on. And there was a lot going on.

I laid on my bed after hanging up with Carol and stared at the ceiling. Why did it matter? Why could I not just let it go and mind my own business? *Because that's what everyone did with me last year, minded their own business.*

I tried to think about who had been in the office with Mr. Hickham and what Sylvie needed to come forward about and whether Nate could have been the one forcing her to come forward. The thoughts rushed through my mind.

Could Nate be blackmailing Sylvie? What would be his endgame? They said he'd done something to someone before. And he was bullying her. That doesn't seem like Nate...but, then again, I've already misjudged him on several occasions.

Mr. Hickham was the principal's assistant, though he called himself the assistant principal, but he was also the assistant football coach. Surely, he wouldn't be involved with a student; that would cost him his job and most likely get him sent to prison. Not probably—definitely.

What if it was two students in his office, and one was roleplaying as Mr. Hickham? Not only was that ludicrous, but it was disturbing. I thought back to that day that I'd walked by the office. Then, I suddenly remembered that Nate had said Sylvie wasn't at practice, and the girls made it a point to rub it in that she'd missed practice several times because of *him.*

Who was 'him'?? Nate? No—that didn't make sense. Nate had been with me in the gym, and according to him, they'd already broken up, and he was trying to make her jealous by meeting with me. Was it Mr. Hickham that she'd missed practice for? Was the 'him' the same 'him' that was her lab partner? Were they different?

My mind was swimming in the deep end with questions when my phone dinged. It was a text from Felix saying that he couldn't come over tonight. As I put the phone down, it practically buzzed out of my hand. It was Nate calling.

"Hello?" I answered with more surprise in my voice than I intended.

"Did I catch you at a bad time?"

"No, sorry. The phone just startled me," I admitted. It felt weird to be talking on the phone to Nate Reinhart.

"Lost in thought? Or busy?" He sounded oddly considerate and not mad.

"Uh…trying to solve a mystery. Sort of."

"A mystery?"

"Sort of," I repeated before swiftly changing the subject. "What's up?"

"What's the deal with Friday?" he asked aloofly.

I raised an eyebrow. "The deal is we have to write an article on the dance," I answered flatly.

"Yes."

"Ok." I felt confused as to why he wasn't mad anymore.

"Do you want to meet there or go together?" he prodded.

"Doesn't matter."

"It does."

This was infuriating! "It does matter, but I don't want to answer that question, because, if I say yes, let's go together, then it makes it seem like I want to go to the dance with you."

"You don't want to go to the dance with me?" Nate clarified.

"Nate—you know you'd never ask me to the dance if you weren't indirectly being forced to go with me."

"You don't know that."

I paused. Was he just being difficult or was he being real? "Have you taken more pain medicine?"

"No, Avery." He sounded irritated again, though to me, the question was valid. In my experience, he'd have to be out of his mind on pain meds to say something like that.

I winced at what was about to come out of my mouth but asked anyway, "Do you think we should go together?"

"Just think, if we're covering it together, we might as well. Plus, I can't drive. So, I need a ride anyway."

"The logic is there, for sure," I said, realizing neither of us wanted to say that we wanted to go with the other.

And then, the thought occurred to me that I could possibly get more information out of him by spending the whole dance with him. Maybe I could figure out what was going on with Sylvie. "Except one thing: I can't drive either."

"You're not sixteen yet?"

"Next week."

"Oh," he answered with barely a hint of disappointment.

"Yep. Well, I guess I'll just see you there, then?"

"Yeah, sure."

There was a pause, and I knew what I needed to say, but, after all the dance nonsense, I hesitated. Plus, maybe he didn't deserve an apology if he was a blackmailer. I felt as though I was about to make a fool of myself yet again if I didn't just hang up the phone now. But I didn't.

"Nate?"

"Yep?"

"Before you go, I just wanted to apologize for the way I acted in the hall today."

"Thanks. I'm not mad anymore."

"Okay. So, see you Friday?"

"Yeah. What are you going to wear?"

"Umm…" *Weird question.* "A dress?"

"You don't know yet? You didn't want to match or anything?"

I laughed to myself and made a face that I was glad he couldn't see. "I'm not that girl, Nate. But thanks for asking."

"Hmm," was his only response.

"Bye, Nate."

"Bye, Avery."

"Are you sure that you don't want me to come with you? This is the first dance you've been willing to go to!"

"Mom, I wouldn't really call this willing," I said with a smirk.

"I know, but you're going to a school function!" she announced in the kitchen to no one.

"It's not a big deal, Mom. I'm just going so I can write the article with Nate later." I shuffled my feet uncomfortably. "Carol and Felix wanted to help pick out a dress. Everyone is a little too excited about this."

"Carol is coming into town just for this?" My mother's

astonishment made her voice rise an octave.

I held up my iPad and pointed to it. "Facetime, Mom. Carol will be on Facetime."

"Oh! Technology...." She shook her head, realizing how silly she had just sounded. "Well, just don't change in front of the iPad...or in front of Felix. That would just be inappropriate."

I rolled my eyes into the refrigerator while I grabbed a water bottle out. "I won't, Mom. You're right; that would be weird."

"I'm surprised Felix doesn't mind helping."

"I asked him to come."

"Why is that?" Mother questioned.

"He picked me to be his friend, so he has good taste?" I smiled mischievously at her and kissed her on the cheek. "We'll be back for dinner."

"Okay, have fun. And don't pick anything orange. You look terrible in orange."

"The zipper is stuck, Felix! And I already feel claustrophobic in this dress. Help me!" I called out from the dressing room, contorting my whole body to try and get the zipper down further so I could be free of the satin and tulle.

"What do you want *me* to do?" he said from the couch in the waiting room that had all the mirrors where I could go loathe myself in all the sparkly dresses he made me try on.

"Get help—I can't get out of this dress!" I felt like I was starting to sweat.

"What do I do?" he asked in a panicked voice.

"Go find a lady in the front." The dress was trying to eat me.

After a moment, Felix returned, panting, and knocked on the door. "I can't find anyone."

"What do you mean? Where is everyone?"

"I don't know, AB, I looked all over. Maybe they went to lunch?"

"Felix, get real. They can't go to lunch with customers in the store!" I panted, trying to breath with my ribs constricted, then wondering how women wore corsets every day.

Stick to the point, Avery Brave.

I had to have help. And, as much as what I was about to say would shock the both of us, I was desperate to breathe again.

"Just get in here and help," I dared to demand.

"What?! I can't come in there, AB. It was inappropriate enough that you wanted me to sit in the rooms with all the mirrors and help you decide. At least the ladies in the front thought so."

"I know, but where are they now?! I need help. I'm completely decent; I just can't get the zipper. And I'm suffocating slowly by way of prom dress. And that is the worst way to die. Now, help me!"

"I can't just leave Carol out here by herself!"

"Don't be ridiculous!"

"I'm not! Why are we shouting?"

"Because I'm starting to hyperventilate and panic in this dress. I can't get out. I told you it was going to be too small."

"I'm coming. Carol's with me."

"Carol, don't tell Mom. She told me not to bring you in the dressing room," I said, looking at Felix.

Felix gave me an odd look, and I realized how erratic I sounded. We both started laughing.

"It's okay for me but not for Carol. That seems backward," Felix said.

"It's not okay for you. But this is a desperate time," I said, tears rolling down my cheeks from laughing.

"Desperate measures and all that."

I nodded, now panting from laughing and from the dress. "Mother said not to let either of you in. We will never speak of this again," I said, giggling with tears still spilling out and my face aching from laughing so hard.

"Well, it might be too small, but it's really cute," Carol said from the tablet.

Felix set Carol down on top of my purse, which was in the chair, and set to helping me with the zipper. He had it almost all the way down when we heard voices coming toward the dressing rooms.

"Shhh." I said, grabbing Felix's arm. He clamped his hand over his mouth and pulled Carol over to us. We stood still like statues against the wall and listened.

Several changing stalls down from us, several voices were talking. One was crying. I quickly recognized them as the same girls from the bathroom the other day: Sylvie, Whitney, and Brooklynn. I mouthed Sylvie's name to Felix, and he nodded.

"He's going to tell everyone," she said through the sobs. "He's going to put it in the paper, he said."

"What paper would publish *that?*"

"What is he going to gain by outing you?"

"He just wants to expose Hickham. He wants us to expose him. And if I don't, he says he'll expose me."

"How's he going to put it in the papers? That's stupid, Sylvie. No one will run that story."

"He says he has an in. And if we don't expose him, then he'll run the other story."

"He wouldn't!"

"You keep saying that!" she said, snorting as she cried.

Felix covered my mouth too and made a "shh" motion to Carol.

"But you guys know what he did to Avery! You know he's capable of a lot worse!"

My knees buckled, and Felix had to catch me against his knees so I didn't fall against the stall and crash to the ground. They were talking about Ace? I had gotten it all wrong. I had assumed it was Nate. But Ace was blackmailing Sylvie.

And that, I believed.

"Speaking of Avery," one of the girls interjected, "did you guys hear that she and Nate are going to the dance together?"

"That can't be true. Nate can't stand her. He told me as much." Sylvie slowed her crying and sneered. "But that doesn't even matter. Can we please focus on what I am gonna do?"

"We've got to find a way to beat him at his own game."

"This isn't a game! If he tells everyone what I did or what Mr. Hickham did…it ruins me either way. And my parents. They'll disown me, I'm sure. I won't get into college, I can't get my scholarship…." She was sobbing hysterically again. "I'll lose everything."

The girls quieted and seemed to console Sylvie for a while, and then one of them asked if she even wanted to look for a dress anymore. She said no, she would come back tomorrow, and they left.

Felix finally let go of me and uncovered my mouth. I let it fall open in shock. I felt him unzip the rest of the dress quietly but hold it together. "There," he said softly.

"Thanks," I mumbled. "I'll be out in a minute."

"Okay. We'll wait for you."

After Felix had gone with Carol on the tablet, I sat down in the blackest tulle I'd ever seen and cried—not hysterically like Sylvie, but I buried my head in my hands and cried.

It had been six months since I had cried about Ace Wentworth, and I hated that I was wasting tears on him again.

And secretly, I didn't know which stung more, what they had said about Ace and me…or hearing that Nate couldn't stand me.

When I finally composed myself and came out of the dressing room, Felix and Carol were waiting.

"First," Felix said straight out of the gate, "I don't think you should listen to what Sylvie said. She was hysterical and can't be trusted. In general."

"Second," Carol piped in, "If Nate has any issue with you, you should wear the red one. If will make him regret any ill feelings."

I smiled. These two knew what to say to make me feel better. I grabbed the red dress and brought it with me to the counter. Carol had a point; if I repulsed Nate Reinhart, I might as well look good doing it.

"No offense to Felix—he's been a good friend to you, Avery," my dad announced from the kitchen. "But I want to drive my daughter to the first Homecoming dance she's going to at All Saints Academy."

I waited by the door, already feeling insecure about this one-shouldered red dress I had chosen. I probably shouldn't have chosen it.

"First and last," I reminded him, checking my hair in the hall mirror. I'd decided against an up-do, opting instead to wear it curly and pulled back on one side in an inside-out braid. I had allowed Mother to do my makeup, though I had micromanaged the entire process, not wanting it to look too heavy. She wanted me to wear bold red lips to match the dress, but I wanted understated, so we went with just gloss. Though she was disappointed.

"We'll see," Dad said slyly as he slid a corsage on my wrist. "We'll see."

"Thanks, Dad. You didn't have to get me a corsage. I'm really just reporting. There won't even be any dancing."

"I didn't know if kids still did this, but I wanted you to arrive in style."

"I don't know what kids are doing. Remember? I don't go to these things."

Mom took some pictures of me on the stairs, and we quickly called Carol so she could see me in the dress she and Felix had picked out. Dad dropped me off, giving me a short pep talk about being nice and working hard but remembering to have fun. He said I deserved some fun.

I kissed Dad's cheek and got out of the car to see Nate waiting for me under the entrance canopy in a black suit with a gold tie. I could see his deep, blue eyes from here and his perfectly styled hair. I bent down to look away and knocked on the window. Dad rolled it down.

"I think I might throw up, Dad," I joked, but I was halfway serious.

"You're called Avery Brave for a reason. Remember who you are."

And with that, he pulled away, leaving me standing in the parking lot with Nate leaning against a pillar, staring at me, holding his crutches in his hands.

Was he thinking how much he couldn't stand me? Was he making jokes about me in his head? Was he wishing he was anywhere else in the world except for here with me?

I pushed a stray curl back and decided that he probably wasn't going to leave the support of the pillar, and I would have to walk toward him. This was the most uncomfortable I'd been in a long time. I remember the feeling I'd had at the dress shop and tried to conjure it up again. *I do look good. Really good.* Felix had told me to give him hell. But I silently scolded myself as I neared him, *No. You have to be nice. Play it cool, like you don't know anything.*

Nate finally pushed off the pillar with his shoulder and tucked his crutches under his arms.

"Hey, Avery."

"Hey," I said, touching my neck and feeling flushed as he said my name, even though he never said it right, and I never seemed to have the courage to correct him. Even though I did to everyone else.

"I got you this," he said. He handed me a corsage that made my Father's pale in comparison. "But I can see you already have one."

He acted like he was rethinking giving it to me, but I took it before he could pull it back. "This one is from my Dad," I said. "He wasn't sure if you were my date or not, so he didn't want me to be without a corsage."

"I should have picked you up. Sorry I can't drive right now. If I would have picked you up, he wouldn't have questioned it."

"It's okay. They know it's an assignment," I said, then immediately regretted the way I'd phrased that. I was always undoing what he was trying to say. I didn't know if this was a date, and I wasn't sure he knew either. But after what Sylvie had said, I just couldn't believe that he would actually ask me to a dance or anywhere else, for that matter, if it wasn't an assignment. And I needed to keep my guard up.

He raised his eyebrows, and his blue eyes narrowed at me like he was scolding me. He opened his mouth to say something but then closed it.

I slid the second corsage on. "I suppose a girl can never have too many flowers." I shrugged, dodging whatever was happening. "Shall we go?"

"Sure." His voice changed back to an aloofness that I was accustomed to.

We went through the entrance, which was filled with glittery stars, moons, and a traditional balloon archway that Carol always made fun of. We walked side by side until we reached the entrance of the picture backdrop. He grabbed my hand and tugged it softly toward the backdrop. We were next in line. I protested with my eyes and shook my head.

"No?"

"Umm...I am just surprised that you..."

"Well, I figured you'd want to experience the whole dance if we were supposed to report on it."

"Oh," I said. His logic was always there, but his motive always eluded me.

The photographer posed us in a traditional dance pose, which Carol and I always made fun of. Nate was behind me with his arms around my waist. For two people who had never so much as touched before, I could feel the awkwardness bleeding out of every pore. I wriggled out of his arms and stood as his side. He looked down at me with questioning eyes, and I saw the photographer's look of concern.

"Just put your hands in your pockets. It's casual," I whispered up at Nate. He did so, and I looped an arm through his, holding my own hand and showing off my two corsages. Then, I nodded at the photographer, who shrugged and got behind his camera.

"Better, right?" I whispered again through a camera-ready smile.

"Much," Nate said before looking stoically at the camera.

As we walked into the dance, Nate said "thanks" nonchalantly where only I could hear. I wanted to mutter something back about being forced to touch someone you couldn't stand, but I didn't; I simply nodded.

For most of the evening, we walked around the dance, observing and occasionally commenting to each other things we noticed. Dress styles were drastically different from last year and slightly more revealing, based on what I'd seen in the yearbook and basic pop culture knowledge. Boys' suits were more tailored and more casual. Song choices were edgy and not what we expected, but we knew "Christian school" didn't mean all things Christian. All the teachers seemed to be present but kept to the fringe of the room and talked amongst themselves.

We stood an arms' length apart and only looked at each other when it was absolutely necessary, which, apparently, it rarely was. Finally, about nine o'clock, I was exhausted of being around him and needed a moment alone. I wanted to call Felix or Carol. I told him I had to go to the bathroom, but on my way, I ducked past the bathroom and went down the west hallway. It was dark and considerably less pungent away from all the sweaty dancing teens. The cool air wafted down from the vents, and I stood directly under one for a moment, letting the air cool me until I got a shiver that shook my spine.

"Why are you calling me when you are with the most eligible running back in school at the homecoming dance?" Carol squeaked.

I ran my hand along the lockers. "I don't know. I just escaped into the hall and needed a friendly voice."

"Is he just the worst? I bet he looks ugly tonight, doesn't he? And he didn't shower? And he's being a complete jerk. I feel so awful for you, dear. You're really taking one for the team here," she said, her tone turning sarcastic.

I giggled a little. "I look terrible too. I should just go home, huh."

'Totally. It's a wash. Never show your face again."

We laughed, and I felt better.

I told her how Nate called me Avery and how I'd been too chicken to correct him. She asked about how the dance was decorated, and she laughed at the balloon arch.

But I stopped mid-sentence as I was telling her about the two corsages when I heard footsteps.

"Gotta go, Carol."

I hung up the call, tucking myself along the wall at the end of the row of lockers, which coincidentally matched my dress, before anyone could see or hear me. I realized as I listened that the footsteps were followed by the sound of crutches. The footsteps slowed, and so did my breathing.

"Avery?" A male voice said my name loud enough to echo down the hall but not so loud that anyone at the dance would have heard. I stilled and was quiet. My heart beat out of my chest, and I was sure that he could hear it.

"Avery?"

I didn't respond, but it was the second time that he called out my name that I recognized Nate's voice. He never called me by my full name.

Why was he looking for me? How had he known I'd ducked the bathroom? For someone who couldn't stand me, he was acting a lot like a date. Not that I'd been on many.

"Avery?" He called out my name again, and I found myself stepping out of my hiding place—not that he could see me. The whole hallway was dark save the emergency lights that blinked every once in a while.

"Yeah?"

"Where are you? I called your name like three times." He sounded concerned.

"I'm over here. Behind the lockers," I whispered harshly, just wishing he would shut up.

I heard his crutches coming my way, and I saw his gold tie reflect the emergency lights as they blinked.

"What are you doing hiding in the hallway?" He stood too close to me, but I know he probably couldn't judge the distance that well in the dark.

"I just—I thought we could both use a—" Deciding not to finish that statement, I opted just to say, "I don't know."

"What's wrong? Did I do something?"

I sighed. "No, I just know that you can't—" I knew I couldn't finish that sentence either without having to explain how I knew that he couldn't stand me. *But why am I so nervous to tell him?*

"Look, I feel like we got off on the wrong foot," he said honestly in the dark.

"Back in the second grade?" I said more bitingly than I meant to.

"Probably." He laughed a little.

He cares that we got off on the wrong foot? That's not someone who can't stand me.

But as I was about to take a breath and say something else, we heard voices coming our way. I grabbed his jacket sleeve and pulled him around the corner into a classroom. His crutches were in one hand, and he hobbled on his good foot, bumping into me awkwardly. We stumbled over each other's feet until he steadied us with his back against the wall.

How is this real?! This can't be happening! I have to get away from him and out of here!

I moved to the side so that we would not be touching, but he put hands on my shoulders and kept me in my place, probably so I couldn't make noise. But my whole body fought against the fact that we were so closely touching.

As the voices grew closer, I recognized Sylvie's voice and let out a small gasp—we both tried to cover my mouth. His large hand was clamped over my mouth first—practically my whole face—and my hand was over his.

I will never recover from this. I have to get out of here. I panicked. *I'll never be able to look him in the eye again. God, please help me. How to get myself in such tight spots?*

I pulled Nate's hand down from my mouth, conscious that his hand had touched my lips, wishing I had never come, never worn this blasted dress, and never come down this hallway.

His hand rested on my bare shoulder now and didn't let go. I wanted to escape it somehow or signal him not to touch me, but I dared not move or make a noise. I even begged my heart to quiet down. We both listened intently, though. I could feel his heart beating as fast as mine, and it was distracting.

"Are you kidding me, Ace?! Now is not the time. We are at a dance."

"But I saw you were talking to him. And I think that you are in over your head! It's time to come forward."

Ace? Ace and Sylvie? If Ace was, in fact, blackmailing Sylvie, then who else had Sylvie been talking to? *It couldn't have been Nate; he's right here with me.*

"I don't know that I really believe he did that stuff," Sylvie argued. "How do I know you didn't just make it all up?"

"You know exactly why, Sylvie."

There was a scuffle of feet, and Sylvie squealed.

"Why would I ever make something up like that?" Ace growled in a way that made my breath catch, and it was then that I realized Nate had an arm around my waist, because his grip tightened.

"Let go...," Sylvie yelped and then cried, "So people would quit talking what you did!"

She let it hang in the darkness, and I knew what she what talking about. Nate squeezed my shoulder. I was fully convinced in that moment that he could, in fact, stand me.

We heard the scuffling continue, but it seemed to be moving

away from us. I imagined Ace dragging Sylvie away while she tried to wriggle free of his bruising grip.

We stood unmoving and barely breathing until we heard no more voices or footfalls.

"Avery—," Nate started softly with a sincerity that made me think it wouldn't be smart for me to stay here in the dark with him, leaning against him.

I tugged on his sleeve again. "Come on. We have to go out there. This could be our story."

I hurried him along. He crutched after me and pulled my arm, stopping in the hallway.

"Plus," I continued, "they are going to do the king and queen soon."

"Ace and Sylvie? That's hardly a story, Avery." Nate seemed to be trying to get me to stay or distract me.

"I know, but I think something else is going on. Ace is blackmailing Sylvie to come forward about something."

"Blackmail? How do you know that?"

I told him all the things I'd overheard in the bathroom and then at the dress shop—all my suspicions, even the ones about him. I even told him what Sylvie had said about him not being able to stand me, which I couldn't believe came out of my mouth, but it was too late to reel it back in.

"You thought I was blackmailing Sylvie?" He sounded astonished.

"Well, you were her boyfriend and her lab partner…."

"And you thought I couldn't stand you?"

"You were friends with Ace! And our interactions thus far have been, well…." I left that hanging.

I didn't have sound logic like he seemed to, but my justifications still seemed to be in my favor.

"Okay, well, let's go," Nate conceded. "Let's see if we can catch Sylvie talking to whoever Ace is mad about. Or jealous of? Or scared of?"

Bewildered, I followed behind him. He didn't seem mad at my theories or false accusations.

"Come on," he insisted, grabbing my hand. "I think it's nearing the last song. Let's get out there and see what we can see or hear."

I asked the obvious question. "Oh? And how do you expect to dance?"

"I'll make it work," he said, and I followed him onto the dance floor. He leaned his crutches on a pillar, and before I knew it, we were slow-dancing. He had his arms around my waist—it felt familiar since he'd just had them around me in the hallway—but he was looking around for Sylvie or Ace. He was good at blending. And I found myself wondering if he'd been blending all along.

Maybe he was never really part of Ace's crowd.

He continued to scan the room, which was good, because, at my height, I wasn't going to see past anyone. He bent low and whispered, "I see Sylvie. I'm going to hobble us over closer. Okay?"

"Okay," I agreed sheepishly, still stunned that we were dancing at all.

Nate grabbed one crutch, and we awkwardly tried to dance closer to the edge of the dance floor. He looked over my head but talked to me. "I'm sorry Sylvie said that about you. I never said that. And it's not true."

"It's okay," I said, not knowing what else to say. I couldn't even bring myself to look up at him.

Soon, I could see Sylvie against the wall. She had clearly been crying. Ace was nowhere to be seen, but Sylvie was rubbing her arm where I knew his grip must have been. In that moment, I wondered not only what Sylvie had gotten herself into with Ace but why. She was in deep; I could tell by the well-masked fear in her eyes. I'd had that same look once. I hadn't masked it with makeup like she did; I'd hid mine well with quick wit and a chip on my shoulder. Ace Wentworth was not one to be trifled with.

Then, Nate said something that shocked me out of my thoughts. "You look amazing tonight," he said, still not looking at me. "I should have told you earlier."

I stared up at him awkwardly in shock till the song slowed and faded away as Principal Sand got up on stage. "As you know," the principal announced, "we do our Homecoming King and Queen with secret ballots here at All Saints. You all have been voting all week, and so, now, our cheerleaders will present our Homecoming King and Queen for 2015!"

The room burst with clapping and cheering. Sylvie, Brooklynn, and Whitney walked up on the stage, looking flawless in their gowns. There was no sign now of Sylvie's earlier distress.

What do you want to bet it's Sylvie, I thought dryly.

Sylvie stepped up to the microphone. "For the 2015 Homecoming King...we have..." She dragged the reveal out while opening the envelope. Then, a pleased smile spread across her lips, and she announced, "Nate Reinhart!"

As Nate let go, I realized that his arms had still been around my waist. He raised his eyebrows at me and crutched toward the stage. Left standing alone, I felt adrift on the dance floor.

Sylvie placed a crown on Nate's head and went to kiss him on the cheek, but he blocked it, which made me curious.

Nate learned over to the mic. "Thanks, everyone," he said briefly, tipping his crown to the gathered crowd.

Whitney handed Sylvie the next envelope, and Sylvie stepped back to the mic. "And now...," she said, "your 2015 Homecoming Queen is...drum roll please..." She opened the envelope, and her mouth fell agape just like the lid of the envelope. She showed it to Whitney and Brooklynn. "This can't be right. Is this a joke?" she muttered a little too close to the mic.

Principal Sand intervened, urging them to just announce it as written. Sylvie grudging stepped back to the mic.

"Somehow...," she started, drawing an *"ahem"* from the Principal behind her, "your 2015 Homecoming Queen is Avery Brave Nightingale." She finished the announcement with a distinct lack of exuberance.

Everyone around me looked at me, smiling, patting me on the back. I returned their smiles with confusion on my brow. Someone urged me toward the stage with a hand on my back. Nate was motioning for me to come toward him with a wide smile on his face. I didn't understand.

The principal offered me a hand, and I found myself on stage with everyone staring at me. Sylvie haphazardly thrust the crown on my head. Everyone clapped and cheered.

I looked to Nate and mouthed, *"It's me?"*

He nodded. My face filled with surprise, and my cheeks flushed.

I was crowned Homecoming Queen.

People voted for me? That didn't make any sense. People didn't even like me. Why would they vote for me?

Nate whispered that we were going to bow, and he grabbed my hand. We bowed to the audience, and they roared with applause.

Principal Sand stepped forward. "Our queen seems to be in shock, so let's show her how happy you are for her as the King and Queen walk to the dance floor for their official King and Queen dance."

Everyone clapped and whistled.

"What is happening?" I asked Nate as we walked to the center of the floor. He handed his crutches off to a friend and balanced rather well without them. He spun me around as best he could and took me by the waist rather firmly. We didn't dance really, more like swayed together considering his foot.

"The prettiest girl, who didn't know she was noticed, just got crowned Queen," he said softly as we began to dance.

Prettiest girl? I thought to rebuff this but didn't. I liked my curly hair, and Mother said I had good skin, even with all my freckles, that would never need makeup to enhance it if I took care of it. I supposed that was good because I rarely thought to put it on. I had bright eyes and a round petite nose and was blessed with decently straight teeth. I was slender but not in any way athletic or voluptuous, that I considered.

All the things that I knew girls my age considered important to be attractive were things I did not possess. *So, me, the prettiest girl?* I hardly thought that was true. Did Nate really think that, or was he simply feeling a little high on adrenaline from the hallway and, now, a crown?

Was he being overly generous in order to gain something? Was he just like Ace and preferred girls who were insecure and easily wooed with attention and compliments?

Was I wrong to have just compared him to Ace? My suspicions were firing, and I took awkwardly deep breath to try and make them stop. Even if he was the same, which I felt at this point was unlikely, I was not the same girl who longed for the attention of the star football player and fell prey to his accolades and affection.

How many times since school started had I realized that I had misjudged Nate Reinhart? I couldn't decide what unnerved me more: Nate Reinhart or the fact that I kept misjudging.

"Sylvie," I answered abruptly.

"What?" Nate looked at me like I was crazy. "No. I meant you."

"Sylvie's leaving," I clarified. "I'm going to go try to catch her."

"Avery—" Nate tried to keep me from going.

Turning back instinctively, I finally corrected him. "It's 'Avery Brave'," I said softly and then continued to walk away from him, still completely bewildered at what had just happened.

"Avery Brave, just leave it. Wait."

I walked out of the front doors, my stomach flip-flopping at the sound of my whole name from his mouth and knowing he couldn't follow very quickly on his crutches. I saw Sylvie sitting on the bench outside, crying. I cautiously joined her on the bench, trying not to startle her.

"Are you okay, Sylvie?" I asked softly.

She looked up from her lap, and the surprise in her eyes was evident. "What do you care? Queen Avery," she added bitingly at the end.

"You just look upset. Do you need a ride? Didn't you come with Ace?"

"What are you, jealous?"

I recoiled and almost fired a retort back at her but realized that she was just hurt and possibly jealous of *me*. "Would you like a ride?" I repeated.

"What, with you and Nate? No thanks."

"I'm not with Nate. My dad is picking me up. We can take you home if you like."

"No," she snapped. "I'll get a ride from M—I mean Whitney."

Was she about to say 'Mister'? I didn't have time to find out because, just then, my phone rang, and Sylvie hurried back inside.

"Hello?"

"Hey, I asked your Dad if I could pick you up instead. I'm on my way now."

"Felix!" I exclaimed. "You are a God-send!"

"I don't know about that, but I am on my way. See you in a minute."

I had so much to tell him. I couldn't wait to see his face when I told him all about Ace and Sylvie in the hallway and when Nate had his hand over my mouth! I hurried out by the curb to wait for him. I texted Carol while I waited and laughed out loud at her comment about the picture pose.

Suddenly, I felt a chill down my spine, and I sensed someone sidling up to me. It was completely different from when Nate had been next to me in the hallway. My skin prickled, and I froze.

"You need to mind your own business, Nightingale." His bitter voice made me cringe. Ace.

Playing it cool, I acted like I didn't know what he was talking about. "I only asked her if she was okay. She looked upset."

"I saw you and Nate come out of that hallway. I know you were lurking."

"Lurking? Who says 'lurking'?"

"I say what I want, and I do what I want." He put an unwelcome and coarse hand on my arm and slid it all the way down to my hand. "And you know it."

I boiled inside. My chest hurt from forcing myself to breathe.

I heard the doors of the school open, and I knew I had a small window of time to make a scene. Now was my chance. I stomped my heel on his foot and shoved him sideways, throwing him off balance.

"Get away from me!" I screamed. Whoever had just come through the doors ran over to us as Ace growled at me and scuttled back inside.

A firm hand steadied me and asked in a concerned voice, "Are you alright, Ms. Nightingale?"

I looked up in surprise and saw Mr. Hickham. He'd been here tonight? I hadn't seen him at all.

"Mr. Wentworth is someone to be careful with," he continued.

In a bold move, I brushed my dress and gathered my clutch, which I had dropped in the scuffle. "He's not the only one," I said coolly.

Mr. Hickham's eyes narrowed, and his brow furrowed, giving me the response I needed.

"You were crowned Homecoming Queen?"

"Don't make it a thing, okay? It's a bit ridiculous."

"But king and queen. It's cute."

"It's not a thing.

"It's a thing."

"It's not," I argued adamantly.

"Well," Felix said, "he was totally your date. You took pictures, you didn't dance with anyone else, and he put his hand on your mouth."

"Shut up, Felix. He was not."

"He was too. Accept it."

"Fine. Whatever."

"So that dress did its thing, then."

I laughed as we pulled up at my house. "Yeah, I guess it did."

"I can't believe you ran out on him after he said that. You have such a way of pissing people off, don't ya?"

"Nobody said he was pissed. And anyway, I may go to All Saints Academy, but I never claimed to be one."

Felix laughed and threw his head back. "Now that's an accurate school motto."

I smiled at the sight of him belly laughing and was glad to

have someone to recap the night with. "Hey, thanks for picking me up," I said. "But starting next week, you won't have to anymore."

Felix scolded me with his brows. "I didn't *have* to pick you up, Avery Brave. I *wanted* to. Can't your friend pick you up from your first school dance?"

I nodded. "I just wish you would have come tonight. Especially with the whole crown thing."

"I would have given anything to see that part. But I don't really do school dances."

"You're above it all—I get it," I joked.

Grinning back at me, he changed the subject. "The ol' birthday is next week?"

"Yep. Wednesday."

"Alright, we'll have that bottle of champagne I have in the backseat for Wednesday then."

I shook my head as I got out of the car. "You're crazy, Felix."

"I have to be crazy to be friends with you!"

"Too true. Goodnight, Felix."

"Night."

When I was halfway up the front step, I heard his car door shut. I spun around to see Felix jogging toward me. I walked back down the steps and met him at the bottom.

"What's up? Did you forget something?"

"No." His face was serious. "I...uh...just needed to tell you something," he said, looking at the ground and fiddling with his keys. He seemed tense or worried, something I couldn't quite read.

"Felix...," I said, grabbing his arm, "what is it? You're being weird."

He wouldn't meet my eyes. "I was talking to my Dad tonight, and he said that we'd been getting to know each other well enough that I needed to tell you something."

"Tell me what, Felix. You're acting strange."

"He told me that I needed to tell you...just that..." He trailed off and paused for a long time.

"Felix! What is it? We're friends, aren't we? What are you holding back?"

"He said you need to be careful," he finished, seeming to change what he had been going to say. "I just want you to be careful."

That didn't seem like something that required so much verbal torture to get out. "Careful? Your dad wants me to be careful? Is that really what he wanted you to tell me?"

"Especially after what you told me that you said to Mr. Hickham. Maybe you should back off for a bit. Lay low. Be careful."

"Okay," I said, taking his concern seriously. I still wondered what it was that he really needed to tell me. "Is that all you need to tell me?" I pressed gently.

"Yeah."

"Okay." I hugged him quickly. "Thanks for looking out for me."

"Welcome," he said sheepishly.

"Night, Felix."

"Night, AB."

I watched Felix's car leave the driveway, then gave a full report to Mother and Dad, who were still reading in the den when I arrived home. Then, upstairs, I slipped out of my dress and into my pajamas. As I crawled into bed and relaxed against the pillow, my phone lit up beside me. I rolled over to see a text from Felix.

SORRY THAT WAS SO WEIRD. I'LL EXPLAIN LATER.

I smiled. He didn't have to explain. I was pretty sure I knew what it was that his Dad was really concerned about.

Just as my bleary eyes were ready to close, my phone lit up again. Expecting another text from Felix, I was surprised to see a text from Nate.

YOU OKAY?

YEA. SORRY I SPILT SO FAST.

IT'S OKAY.

I'LL EXPLAIN LATER.

I HAD FUN TONIGHT.

I smiled, even though I was so tired that the light from the screen made me squint. I had one boy in my life who thought he was full of surprises, but, really, I had him pegged from the beginning. Then I had another boy who I'd thought I had pegged but who continued to baffle me at every turn. And then, there was one boy who seemed to be at the center of a very scandalous mystery.

ME TOO, I replied to Nate and fell asleep.

6.

A few years ago, our downtown could have been called "small town" or "quaint." Now, while it still held a certain picturesque humility, it had grown more diverse, artistic, and downright interesting. A water fountain surrounded by an expertly coifed flowerbed and large oak trees formed the center of the town square.

Friendly faces sat out on patios enjoying their evening meals as they listened to music across the lawn. Shopkeepers closed their shops and headed home as the sun dipped low between the streets that intersected here.

Nate and I sat in a booth by a window at a burger place on the corner, and I watched the shopkeepers disappear as we ate.

"You said that?" Nate asked and almost dropped his fries out of shock. "Out loud?"

"Yeah." I shrugged, remembering a few things that Nate had said out loud that night too.

I probably should have felt bad for saying what I did to Mr. Hickham, but frankly, I didn't.

Nate shook his head and took another bite of his burger. We were at the Burger Shack working on the article, and Nate had said he'd heard about Ace threatening me at the dance. I'd told him what Ace had said and everything that had happened after that.

"Can't believe I didn't know any of that happened. Where was I?"

"Standing there in shock that the princess just ran out on you," I joked, then immediately regretted it because I'd inadvertently cast him as Prince Charming.

I chided myself. *Wow, really cramming your foot in your mouth lately, eh, AB?*

Nate's eyes widened at my remark, and a smirk pulled at his mouth. He chuckled slightly. "You are the Queen, remember. Not the princess," he joked slyly.

I could feel the heat rise in my cheeks and debated dashing to the bathroom. Brushing waves of hair from my face, I could tell the blush was simply spreading as Nate continued to watch me, eating his fries.

"What?" I asked laughingly.

"Nothing. I—um—I just can't believe you said that to Mr. Hickham."

"I was testing him," I said, moving on flawlessly, glad to get past the Queen conversation. "I needed to see if he'd react and if his reaction would betray him. And it worked. I think we can assume he's involved somehow."

"We?"

"The royal we, I meant," I corrected swiftly. "Me."

He took another bite and looked out the window. After he was done chewing, he looked back at me with serious eyes. "I just think maybe it's not a good idea to get involved. I mean, I think there's more going on than you know...and—"

I slid sideways against the wall in the booth. "Nate, I know you're kind of new to this reporter/newspaper thing, but part of being a reporter is uncovering and exposing things that other people don't...or won't."

"No, I get that. But one minute, we're reporting on the current dress styles and dances, and the next minute, we're trying to expose some seedy business that's possibly going on with students and coaches. Don't you think that, if this is real, you need to go to the police or something?"

I studied his worried face. *Is he concerned about what we'd find? Or me? My safety? Or is he more worried about the fallout for his reputation if he helps me expose it? Or is he hiding something different altogether?*

"Nobody asked you to help me, Nate," I said breezily. "We can just do the school functions and fluff pieces. I can go at this alone. But," I added graciously, "your warning is duly noted."

"Okay," he surrendered. He finished his burger, and we sat in awkward silence until Felix unexpectedly popped in through the front door.

"Well, what do we have here?" he said, surprised to see us in the booth and giving me a mischievous grin.

"School assignment," I jumped in to say before Nate could say anything.

"Hey, Felix." Nate nodded at him in his usual aloof manner.

"Hey, Nate."

"What are you doing here, Felix?" I asked in a chipper voice.

"My parents sent me out to pick up food."

"Cool," I said, waiting for something more, but I sat smiling at him awkwardly for a moment before he made a move to leave.

"Call ya later?" he asked as he walked away.

"Yep," I said feeling a sudden void at the table without him.

"You guys together?" Nate asked, looking at me curiously.

I laughed out loud, probably a little too loud. "No! Gosh no."

He looked at my skeptically. "Didn't you just say that he picked you up from the dance the other day?"

"Yeah? So?" I wondered how he knew that.

He leaned way over the table and was encroaching on my side of the booth. "So, you ran out on me at the dance, and Felix picked you up. You don't see how that looks? And every time I see you at school, you're with him."

Irritated, I grabbed my purse and started to slide out of my seat. "First of all, I didn't run out on you, because we weren't on a date. Second of all, I don't know what it matters to you how things look…." I paused to take a breath, trying not to get too fired up.

"Is there a third?" he retorted meanly.

"Actually, there is, Nate. Thirdly, Felix is not interested in me. We're just friends."

"You've got to be blind, Avery. He is always around. I don't believe girls and boys can truly be 'just friends'."

"Of course, they can, Nate."

I stood and, for once, towered over him, bracing myself on the table, and whispered in a low but fierce tone, "It's really none of your business, and, frankly, I don't even see why you care. If you want to know so bad, ask him yourself, Nate Reinhart." I spat out his name at the end.

His eyes widened as his face drained of color. For the second time, I stormed away from him and caught Felix on the way out the door. He whipped around with the to-go bag in his hand and whacked me with it. I yelped and jumped back with a startled laugh.

"Sorry," he said with wide eyes, assessing me. "You okay?"

"Give me a ride home?" I asked, still fuming.

"Sure. What happened with Inspector Handsome over there?"

I silently followed Felix to his car and got in.

"Ugh," I sighed finally as I buckled in, and we pulled away. "He's impossible and infuriating and…ill-mannered."

"Anything else you want to add to that alliteration?" Felix laughed as we drove away.

"Yeah. He's ornery and obtuse."

"I don't think you did that right," Felix teased.

I shoved his shoulder. "Stop. I'm really mad. I'm not trying to alliterate."

"I don't think that's a word, AB."

"I don't care," I said, laughing because he was frustrating me so much.

"Sorry. I'll stop. I can tell you are upset," he said, softening. "Want to talk about whatever it was that just happened back there? Because everything seemed fine when I was over there, and then it dived south pretty quickly."

I sighed loudly. I wasn't ready to have this conversation with Felix. I was sure it was what he'd been trying to tell me the night of the dance. And why he hadn't called since then. But, in this moment, I knew I didn't have the right words to say, and I didn't want to hurt Felix or jeopardize our comfortable friendship.

I knew not everyone at Saints would react in a similar manner when and if they found out, so I shot up a little "arrow prayer," as Mother called them, before I spoke.

God, help me do this well. I need your words, not mine. I'll mess it up for sure.

"Nate thought you and I were together," I admitted, feeling the air get sucked out of the car. "And he wouldn't let it go."

If it is possible to go pale and flushed at the same time, that's was Felix's face did. He didn't look at me, just kept staring out at the traffic. He took a steadied breath and said, "There's something I need to tell you. I tried to tell you the night of the dance."

"It's okay, Felix."

"No, my dad was worried about you thinking…"

I tried to preempt the "let down easy" he thought he needed to do. "Felix, you don't need to worry about that."

"No, I do. My dad thinks we've been spending so much time together that you might think…I have feelings for you."

Oh gosh. Stop. "Felix—stop."

"Don't get upset. Let me finish."

"Felix!" I raised my voice. "I know you're not interested me. It's okay."

"I don't want you to feel rejected though. You are really gorgeous and smart and funny—"

I put my hand on his arm. "Felix. It's okay. I know you're gay."

He swerved abruptly and stopped the car on the shoulder of the road so fast that we almost spun out. He looked at me with wild eyes that were mixed with confusion and surprise, and he looked as if he couldn't breathe.

"I'm not gay!" he exclaimed finally. "How did you know?"

I cocked my head to the side. "I'm confused. You're not?"

"How did you *know?*"

"Apparently, I didn't know anything, because you just said you're not."

"I'm not!" He was exasperated.

"I'm so confused," I said, shaking my head in bewilderment.

He turned the car off and shifted in his seat to face me. I tucked one leg under me and did the same. He took a deep breath. He was about to tell me all the surprises he thought he was guarding so well.

"It's not that I'm attracted to boys. I'm not. At least I don't think."

"So…you're not gay?" I clarified.

"Just let me get through this. It's complicated." I nodded, and he continued, "I also don't feel attracted to girls. I just don't have any interest either way."

A small smirk tugged at my mouth, and I fought it but couldn't seem to help it. He looked surprised and curious at my forming reaction.

"So…you're asexual?" I let my smile all the way out and teased him, hoping it would put him at ease and break the tension. He laughed.

"Yes, Avery. I'm a coldblooded Komodo dragon." He glared at me mischievously.

I giggled and covered my mouth.

"I know it sounds bizarre, but it's as if I'm not sexual *at all.*"

"It's not bizarre. It sounds kind of nice actually. Not having to worry about all of that. Nate said that girls and boys couldn't be just friends. And I said that they could. If only everything wasn't so darn romantic, they could be. And see, it works this way."

"Shut up. You're just mocking me."

"No, I'm not. Not to get all biblical on you, but, in the Bible, Paul the apostle talks about how it would be better if a man could remain unmarried and that he should only really get married if he couldn't take the sexual pressure and purity. So, I think that maybe it's not bizarre; it's a blessing. You can actually think objectively instead of with your hormones."

"You make me sound like a robot."

"I don't mean to."

"My dad is thinking of having a lot of tests run to see if there's something wrong with me."

"There's nothing wrong with you, Felix," I said, reaching for his hand.

"Well, he thinks so," he mumbled as something sad flashed across his eyes that he didn't speak but I saw.

"Well, I'm sorry he makes you feel wrong or broken. Would it be better or worse for him if you were one or the other?"

"Tough question." He shrugged.

"I know."

He paused for a moment and turned the car back on. "So, you thought I was gay? And that was ok?"

I smiled at him without missing a beat and answered, "Let me put it this way: you're a human and my friend first and foremost. Even if you were gay, we'd still be friends."

"You're one of a kind, Avery Brave Nightingale," Felix said with amazement in his voice as he drove off the shoulder and headed for my house.

As I got out of the car, I leaned back in the window. "Tell your parents that it's my fault their burgers are cold now."

"They won't mind. My Dad will be glad that we finally talked about all this."

"I appreciate that he cares about me feeling misled."

"Yep. He's Colonel Cares-a-lot," he said facetiously.

"See you tomorrow."

"Hey! It's birthday-Wednesday tomorrow. What are we doing?"

I shrugged. I honestly hadn't thought too much about it.

"Well, we'll live it up. For sure. You only turn 16 once! See ya tomorrow."

As I went inside, I checked my phone and saw that I had three missed calls. Two from Nate, no doubt feeling guilty for the way he'd acted at the restaurant, and one from what I recognized as a gym pay phone, which Carol used to call me from when she had volleyball practice before she owned a cellphone. *Who would be calling from the school? Especially this late in the day?*

I ignored all the texts and went inside to call Carol and tell her everything, wishing desperately she could be here for my birthday.

My dark corner was filled with balloons the next morning, which made it rather cheery instead of dark. But by first track, I'd been called to the office because of them. They were a "fire hazard" and got confiscated until after school. *Typical.*

"Mr. Hickham is just sticking it to you on your birthday, you know," Felix teased as we walked down the hall.

"Yeah. He really got me." I nudged him. "Thanks for the balloon entourage, though. Super great start to my birthday."

"More to come, birthday girl."

"You spoil me, good sir!" I shouted after him. When I turned back to go in the classroom, Mr. Knight and Nate were standing at the end of the hall, pensively waiting on me. They motioned for me to join them. *This doesn't look like birthday fun.*

"Avery, we need to talk," Mr. Knight said vaguely and ushered us both into his classroom. "Have a seat."

"What's this about, Mr. Knight?"

"Rumors are going around, Avery."

"Rumors always go around. This is high school," I retorted. Nate shot me a look.

"Well, these rumors are that you have a theory about a certain assistant coach/principal and are trying to investigate that theory."

"How do these gossips even know about that to be able to spread said rumors?" I shot Nate the same look he'd just given me. "But, for the record, I don't have a complete theory just yet."

"Now, don't blame it all on Nate. Though he did come to me out of concern, I'd already heard it from several others."

How?

"Am I doing anything against the law or school policy?"

"No, just dangerous. And questionable."

"What's dangerous? To me, what is potentially happening with Mr. Hickham is what is dangerous. And Ace Wentworth is dangerous."

"Exactly. Wait—what does Ace have to do with this? No, you know what? Don't tell me that. You don't want to get caught in the crossfire of whatever is going on just for the sake of the story."

"And," Nate chimed in, "you couldn't verify any of this theory unless you got really involved. And that could be risky. *Plus*, we really just need to report this. I'm surprised you haven't before now."

I stood up from my desk and pointed out the door. "Guys, are you telling me that, if an adult is involved with teens in any sort of inappropriate manner, and other students are blackmailing other students, it's not our responsibility to expose that and help bring him to justice?"

"No, just that you need to leave it to the proper authorities," Mr. Knight corrected calmly.

"And, what, I'm not capable of solving this before handing it to said authorities?" I raised my voice a little. "What...because I'm a girl? Or because I'm a student? Because either way, that is offensive. And I know that we need to turn this over to the authorities; I'm not just not sure of any of it yet. I want to be sure before we do."

"Is this about last year?" Nate asked cautiously.

"Maybe," I answered before I fully realized what he'd asked. I looked down at my hands, which had been wringing, and digested what he was asking. "Yes," I said finally. "I suppose it does. I was a victim of injustice last year even though I had proof. I was the proof. So, I'm hesitant to run to the police and the law again."

They both stared at me blankly for several moments before Mr. Knight replied, "You're right, Avery Brave. Just give me some time to think this through before you move any further on it. We're going to have to go about this in a very delicate way. Okay?"

"Okay," I said with relief. They weren't quite supportive, but they were at least not trying to talk me out of it anymore—and at least we all knew why I was so adamant about this. Especially me.

Nate nodded but didn't meet my eyes. I had never returned his call, and apparently now we were both upset with each other.

I agreed to do as Mr. Knight asked and give him some time before I dug any further, but I couldn't help it if I overheard anything else, now, could I? But I wasn't going to camp out in the bathroom to see if I could catch Sylvie in there. Today was my birthday, and I intended to have fun.

But first, I wanted to go look at the phone in the gym and maybe find a clue as to who would have called me.

I slipped into the gym and tried not to *clip-clop* down the stairs of the stands. The payphone was on the opposite wall from the coach's office. I listened to the herd of cleats exit the locker room, followed by the sound of Nate's crutches. I waited along the corner till the room was still.

The payphone was black and looked like it weighed a hundred pounds. The coin return was empty, and the receiver was clean. I looked around and tried to gauge the distance between all the closest doors and studied the floor for any dropped scraps or threads.

"Look who came looking for me." Ace's gravely whisper froze me in place and sent a rippling, radiating shiver through my body. I forced my body to spin on my heel and face him, my face blank as a stone but my blood pumping.

"Got my message, I see."

He called? "Message?" I said coldly.

"You came, didn't you? I knew you'd come."

This was trap. *I need to get out of here,* I thought with alarm. *How can I away from him?* I started planning my escape, knowing I couldn't get up all the stand stairs fast enough. The loading door was up and was probably the closest door, though I'd have to go fast to get away and close enough to yell for help.

"I didn't know it was you, Ace. I wouldn't be here if I had known."

"Oh. I see how you're playing it now. The queen is coy, is she?"

"No," I said, starting to panic as he took a step closer.

"You're bold to come in the gym alone after school looking for, what...clues? Or did you come looking for something more, maybe?"

"Don't come any closer, Ace Wentworth."

"What are you going to do? Cry wolf again? Like you did at the dance? I'd like to see you try that again. See what happens. Oh, wait—nothing. Like the time before. Like last year. Who are they going to believe?"

My fists tightened, not out of aggression but out of necessity. I needed to force my courage to kick in and help me run. My heart raced, and my breath was thin and rapid. I did feel powerless, but I wished for the power to enforce. I envied the strength to demand justice. I craved the leverage to ruin him.

My fists tightened more, and my nails dug into my hand. I couldn't fight him effectively; I didn't know how. But I felt like it. And I knew I needed to run.

Now.

I spun on my heel again and accidentally crow-hopped a little before bolting across the gym.

"You can't outrun me, Nightingale!" he shouted after me.

I got to loading door faster that I'd thought I could and jumped down, landing on my feet and sprinting around the front of the school, not checking to see if Ace had followed.

Ace had called. He wanted to rattle me. *It worked,* I thought, trying to slow my breathing but instead starting to cry. But when I was sure I'd lost him, I stopped running. I had managed to out run Ace which was something I didn't think I was capable of. But that wasn't the point, I shook my head and cleared my throat. I refused to let him get to me. I refused to cry about it.

Ace wanted to rattle me. And I doubted it was just about last year. He was more involved than I thought. Maybe Mr. Knight was right; maybe I did need to be careful. And yet, I was on to something here.

And I was done feeling powerless.

"Guess you don't need a ride now," Felix said, checking out my new-to-me land cruiser.

"Nope," I said, happy as a lark. My mother had arranged for Felix to come for dinner and had set a place at the table for Carol on Facetime, which she still didn't understand. We'd watched my favorite movie in our theater room complete with popcorn and candy and slushies. And then, my Dad surprised me with a car in the driveway. It was a perfect birthday, and I was glad I got to spend it both physically and digitally with my best friends.

I said goodnight to Mom and Dad and thanked them for a great sixteenth birthday, then flopped on my bed. I smiled, thinking back over the fun things Felix had done for me that day. I'd gotten the balloons back at the end of the day, and they were now tied to my desk chair in my room. He'd had flowers delivered at lunch along with a cake, and he'd had the choir sing "Happy Birthday" over the intercom.

But reliving the fun from today was interrupted by my phone vibrating. It was Nate.

I'VE BEEN TRYING TO CALL FOR DAYS.

    I KNOW

I WANT TO APOLOGIZE.

    I KNOW.

FELIX INVITED ME TONIGHT BUT I FIGURED YOU WOULDN'T WANT ME THERE

    OH

ANYWAYS, SORRY. AND HAPPY BIRTHDAY

    THANKS

NIGHT, AVERY BRAVE

    NIGHT

"I'm just surprised you'd invite him, that's all."

"But you're not mad?" Felix clarified while I tried to get my locker open.

"No, just surprised."

"Is that all he said?" Felix prodded.

I finally heard the latch unlock, and I opened the door. "Yeah, should he have said something more?"

A folded piece of paper fell out of my locker, which must have been why the door was sticking.

"A note? How very old-school of someone. And no, I was just curious how far this text conversation went."

I gave Felix a "that's stupid" look and unfolded the piece of paper. In black marker, the words looked auspicious and angry with a hard slant that put indentions in the paper with the start of each new word.

I showed it to Felix, who read it aloud but quietly: "Quit while you can. You have NO idea what you're getting into."

His mouth made a silent "wow," and he handed the note back to me. Someone was threatening me, but who? Ace again? Most likely, after the other day. I quickly went down my mental list of all the people that knew about the alleged blackmail. Mr. K., Mr. H., Nate, Ace, Sylvie…

"You okay?"

I was lost in thought and forgot we needed to get to class. "Oh. Yeah, sorry. I was just thinking about who it could be from."

"You're not worried, though?"

"No, not really. I mean, I was scared the other day in the gym—but I'm done being afraid. Maybe it means I'm on the right track?"

"Or maybe it just means Ace is a bully. AB, you scare me."

"In a fierce kind of way or in a clown kind of way?"

"Don't even talk about clowns! That's just mean. Now I'm going to be thinking about scary clowns all day. You're rude, Avery Brave. Rude."

I giggled as we parted ways down the hall. It was good that we didn't have any classes together, because we'd surely be in trouble the entire time.

I needed to get my notebook and make notes. I snuck into the cafeteria, which was deserted except for the ladies who were busy in the kitchen getting ready for lunch, which was in an hour. I had enough time to sit down and think this through.

I wrote down my suspect list and, beside each name, I wrote a "what if" question about what they would have to lose if I was right.

WHAT IF NATE WAS JUST AS INVOLVED AS ACE? HE IS/WAS FRIENDS WITH ACE AND WAS DATING SYLVIE.

WHAT IF MR. KNIGHT KNOWS MORE THAN HE'S LETTING ON?

WHAT IF FELIX HAD BLOND HAIR? —I had nothing on Felix.

WHAT IF ACE DID SOMETHING ILLEGAL? IF HE GOT CHARGED FOR SOMETHING ELSE, WE MIGHT BE ABLE TO TAKE HIM DOWN FOR THE CHARGES THAT HE AVOIDED LAST YEAR. He would certainly try to scare me off the scent if I was getting to too close. Was he possible scared? (That was a stretch, but this was a what-if game I was playing.)

WHAT IF MR. HICKHAM IS TRYING TO SHUT ME UP BECAUSE HE REALIZED AFTER THE DANCE THAT I'M ON TO HIM?

BUT AM I ON TO HIM? WHAT DO I EVEN KNOW? Did the pieces equal anything concrete? Not really; it was circumstantial. I needed to bounce this off someone safe. Who could I trust? Not anyone on the list, really. Even Felix was too concerned to be objective.

I decided to talk to the guidance counselor. I faked some emotions at the front office and begged to see her. She smiled at me, knowing I wasn't really having a crisis.

"What's up, Avery?" she said, leaning on her desk and removing her glasses.

"Hey, Ms. Midler."

"What's the fake crisis about?"

"I need to ask you some hypothetical questions."

"You know you don't have to have a breakdown to make an appointment with me."

"Yeah, but I was already skipping class, so I need a valid excuse for later."

She shook her head and laughed. "You're good, but I'm going to pretend you didn't just say that."

I smirked. "Can I ask you some questions?"

"Hypothetically?"

"Yes."

"For an article?"

"Hypothetically." I shrugged.

"Shoot."

I got my notebook out to make notes. "Hypothetically, have you had any students in here with legal problems?"

"First of all, you know I can't answer that. Second, this is high school, Avery. What do you mean 'legal problems'?"

"Okay, I'll reword. But, for the record, this is an affluent school; people sue their parents and whatnot all the time."

She looked at me skeptically. "Maybe, but this is a *Christian* school."

"I think you and I both know that doesn't mean much," I mumbled, "but that's for another time. Have you had any students having problems with teachers?"

"Students always have problems with teachers." She laughed. "This is high school. And you know I can't really answer that."

I pursed my lips. This would be tricky. "Okay, how about I come at this from a different angle." I tapped my pen on the notebook and thought until it came to me. "Hypothetically, if you heard from a student that a teacher was engaging in something inappropriate or illegal, what would be your required action?"

Ms. Midler's eyes widened, and she leaned over her desk and folded her arms. She wasn't upset, but she was serious. "Avery, I don't know what you've heard or gotten yourself into, but those kinds of accusations can cause a lot of uproar."

"I am not accusing anyone. I simply asked a hypothetical question."

"Okay, okay. *Hypothetically*, if I had heard this from a student, I would be forced to report it to the proper authorities. I don't think I have to tell you this, Avery, but in any school, inappropriate behavior on behalf of a teacher or illegal dealings are taken very seriously and can cause a lot of damage to whomever is involved." She hung on the word "whomever," implying it damage teachers and students involved as well.

"Message received."

She put her glasses back on. "And you know I have to make note of this conversation in your chart."

"That's fine. A paper trail may be helpful at some point," I said fairly snarkily.

She scribbled on a note and shoved it across the desk. "Run along now, get back to class. But keep me in the loop. I can help—okay?"

I nodded and headed down the east hall only to practically run into Ace, who was coming out the science lab.

"Watch yourself, Nightingale!" he gruffed but quickly changed his tone and taunted me further. "Can't outrun me. Can't get enough, eh, Nightingale?"

I just glared at him and continued on down the hall. I could hear the scuffle of his feet coming after me. My heart beat faster as I felt him catching up with me.

I could hear the sneer in his voice as he whispered in my ear and grabbed my arm, just like he had at the dance. "You're always getting in over your head and getting yourself hurt. Aren't you, Avery Brave?! May not want to go too many places alone anymore." He let go of my arm with a shove. "But hey, if something were to happen, maybe you could prove it this time."

He let the low blow slice through the air and hit me right where it hurt. But he wasn't done.

"Speaking of proving it, maybe you should ask your little reporter friend about what he's hiding. Tell him I can prove it's his."

He shoved me as hard as he could, and his verbal jab knocked the wind out of me. I landed on the cold, hard tile floor, my notebook sliding at least five feet away from me. All I could hear was the sound of Ace laughing cruelly and jogging away. I sat up and realized I had tears sliding down my face, and it registered how ironic it was that I had faked a crisis not thirty minutes ago only to be having a real one now.

"Avery?!" Nate's voice echoed in the hallway as he crutched toward me.

Fabulous. "It's 'Avery Brave'," I muttered angrily.

"Are you okay? What happened?" he said, dropping his crutches and balancing on one foot to lean over toward me.

I shook my head. I didn't want him to be the one that found my helpless on the floor, crying.

"Avery. Come on, let me help you up," he said, taking my arm, which I snatched back from him harshly.

"I don't need your help."

"Is this about the note that you found? Is someone after you?"

Felix! I could kill you! Why does he keep telling Nate stuff? I glared at Nate as I stood up on my own and walked over to retrieve my notebook. He followed, even though I was treating him terribly.

"I just bumped into Ace. And I fell." I brushed myself off, feeling dirty from the floor or shameful from the lie. "I'm fine." Somehow, in that moment, I was reverting back to old habits.

Nate studied me as if he didn't believe me. I knew that he'd heard that story before, because I'd told it several times before concerning Ace—not to Nate directly, but I was sure he'd heard some version last year. And whether I said it so he would know or whether I thought I'd really get the lie past him, I wasn't sure.

Nate motioned for me to follow him, and I shook my head.

He motioned again, crutching toward the supply closet. *I am not about to go in a supply closet with Nate Reinhart. What was this, a teen sitcom?!*

I shook my head again at which point he grabbed my hand gently and pulled me over to the door.

"I need to tell you something. Just trust me."

"I'm not going in there with you. Do you think I'm an idiot?"

"Avery. I need to talk to you."

"We're alone in the hallway, Nate. Talk."

"Avery, please…" He looked desperate. Maybe I was about to get a confession out of him. Whether it was curiosity or stupidity, it didn't matter. I let him pull me into the supply closet. It was dark for a moment, and I had a sudden flash of being pushed up against the wall the night of the dance with his hand over my mouth, hearing his heart beat fast. My face flushed, and I rethought my decision to be in here with him and tried to push past him.

"No. I shouldn't be—I have to go," I said, trying to feel my way past him in the dark. He tried to get me to stop with a hand on my stomach just as he also found the light switch. We stood toe to toe with his hand on my stomach, and I knew that, if I looked up, his face would be entirely too close to mine. I scrambled away from him and folded my arms.

"Aright, you've got me in here. Now what?"

"I need to tell you something."

"That you're the one who sent the note?" I accused fiercely.

"What? No!" he protested defensively. "But…I know what part of this is about."

I took a step back. Even though I'd considered him a suspect, I still felt betrayed. "Which part? How long have you known?"

"I know what Ace is threatening Sylvie about."

"Do tell before the bell rings and we're stuck in here all of lunch."

"Last year, when you and Ace broke up…"

I already didn't like where this was going. I shook my head

and headed for the door again, but Nate held up a hand to stop me.

"Just hear me out. I know you walked in on Ace with someone. Right?"

I nodded painfully.

"It was Sylvie. They've been on again, off again since you guys were together. I didn't know until—well, that's why we broke up at the beginning of the year."

"Fine. It was Sylvie. What does this have to do with Mr. Hickham?"

"I don't know yet. But there's more to Ace and Sylvie."

And it was then that Ace's voice echoed in my mind—my little reporter friend was hiding something.

"Ace made Sylvie have an abortion."

I gasped. *That's was he was hiding? Sylvie was pregnant?* Ace had said he could prove it was "his". Who was "he"? The baby was Nate's? And before I could stop the second accusation from flying out of my mouth, it escaped: "It was your baby, wasn't it?"

He looked as though the crutches might give out on him and that I was purple and red spotted with green teeth or something. "No! Why would you think that—we never—I never— Why would you think it's mine?"

Trying to push past the vulnerability he'd just admitted to me in the supply closet, I stumbled over my words just as much as he had. "Ace said—I just assumed... I'm sorry."

"Ace is trying to make Sylvie say that it was mine. But it's not even possible."

Okay! Enough indirect virginity talk. "Why would he say it's yours if it's not? How do you know all of that? Why does he need to blame you anyway?"

"He's Ace. He likes to brag. He has a way of dodging the consequences of his actions."

Nate looked at me in a way that made me feel like I was translucent, and he could see inside of me. He *had* known that I was lying.

"When you lied to me out in the hall, I knew that what I'd always suspected about the rumors from last year were true. Ace told very different versions of what happened and what you were like. But the blindfold was ripped off when I learned about him and Sylvie. He's a dangerous liar."

I looked at my feet, feeling the heat from my embarrassment and shame rise from my stomach and spread to the ends of every hair.

"And so, what's true?" I mumbled, too afraid to look at him.

"That's there's much more to the story than what everyone knows. You've been through a lot."

I shook my head as hot tears spilled out of my eyes. *I am in a supply closet crying in front of Nate Reinhart. Could anything be more humiliating?*

"I didn't mean to upset you. I was trying to tell you that I can see now that Ace was lying last year."

"I don't want to talk about it," I said flatly.

"You don't have to." He crutched a little closer to me. I was already against the shelves with the toilet paper rolls and couldn't scoot any further from him. "Just know that, if you ever do, I'll believe you."

I forced a cruel scoff. "Why would I tell you? You're friends with him. I see the way you guys make fun of me in keyboarding and in the hallway. Just because we have to work together doesn't mean that I trust you. Any more than him."

"Why do you think I was hanging around him? He was threatening me that he'd tell the whole school and my parents that Sylvie had aborted my baby."

I sniffed and relaxed slightly. "How long has he been threatening you? Why did you pretend not to know what was going on?" I narrowed my eyes. "And what does all this have to do with Mr. Hickham?"

"I can't figure that out yet. All I can figure is that the abortion is the leverage that Ace is threatening Sylvie with if she doesn't come clean about whatever else they're hiding. He threatening to go to the paper about the pregnancy if she doesn't go to the paper first with the other story."

"What are we, Beverly Hills? Nobody cares. And wouldn't that expose their little secret? Why would they risk doing that for another secret?"

"Well, don't forget, he was forcing Sylvie to tell everyone it was mine. So, unless she comes clean about something else, he's threatening to ruin her reputation and probably her college career—and mine too. Neither of us would get into the schools we want with a scandal like this. Our parents would most likely believe it and then cut us off or disown us from the shame it would bring on the family."

"I guess I see why you didn't tell me at first."

"Sin is like buckshot; it's got a wide radius."

"Buckshot? Good analogy," I said, distant and distracted as I tried to think of a way to find out what else Ace and Sylvie were hiding.

"Thanks."

We stood there, facing each other—sort of staring at one another, though we were both thinking and not directly looking into each other's eyes. I had no idea what time it was or how long we'd been in the closet. Had we missed lunch or the bell ringing?

"I'll try to keep my ear to the ground in the locker room and see if I can come up with any leads," Nate offered, which surprised me.

"I thought you didn't want me to pursue this."

"No, I don't. I didn't want you to find out about all this. But it seems to be coming to you, so I want to help. I've got the locker room access to Coach; we'll see if that leads anywhere. Maybe keep your head down for a while. If Ace is the one who wrote the note, then make him think that he got to you and that you're letting it go."

"What will that do?"

"Make him or them slip up. If he thinks he's bested you, he's bound to betray himself at some point. He can't help but boast about himself and what he gets away with."

I didn't even want to know what he'd boasted about last year. Ace Wentworth was a weasel and bully, and, as much as I wanted to punch him in the face, I'd be glad to steer clear of him.

"I just can't understand why you were in the supply closet with him, Avery. I just don't think that looks good at all," Mom said, concerned, as she past the cobbler to Dad. I had told them the entire story of that day at school.

Dad took the cobbler from Mom and set it down, not taking any. I looked at Mom, who made an "eek" sort of face. Dad was still stuck on the part where Ace had shoved me, I knew.

"Dad, I know we could make a thing over Ace shoving me and harassing me really, verbally, but if he's involved in this the way that Nate says, then, if we let things play out and blow up in his face—"

"Avery!" Mom exclaimed.

"Fine, maybe he got off because his father paid the judge off last time, but maybe he couldn't escape this. Maybe we could finally take him down."

Dad took a long and controlled breath before he spoke. "Avery, as much as I'm having to hold myself back from storming the Wentworths' front gate, I don't want you to get into this revenge game. I know that's not what God wants us to do. We have to figure out how to forgive them."

That was not what I thought was going to come out of his mouth. I had anticipated having to talk him down from showing up at the school and pinning Ace against the lockers. I thought he was furious, and I suppose he was, but he was more concerned about my heart and what God wanted for me than he was about Ace getting what he deserved.

And I guess my face showed my surprise, because he continued, "I know that's not how we handled things last year, but we've all grown from that. Right?"

I nodded.

"And I won't ever let you feel like I don't want to charge the field, knock someone's block off, or grab my gun on your behalf…but I want to honor God with how I handle sin committed against us."

I smiled. While no one else I knew said "knock someone's block off," it was comforting to know that he would want to knock Ace's block off. But it was more of a comfort to me that my Father was a man of integrity.

I couldn't help also thinking about proof. We needed proof. And lots of it.

"Thanks, Dad. I do need to work on forgiving him," I said with half-hearted resolve.

"And that's not to say that you shouldn't still stand up for a student if a teacher is doing something inappropriate or unfair. It's appalling to think that could actually be happening at All Saints, and I hope that is not the case. But you follow your discernment. But do it cautiously."

"Yes, sir."

"And the minute you need our help, you let us know. We'll back you up anytime you need."

"Thanks, Dad. Mom, you too. You guys are the best."

While I knew what Mother wanted was a group hug, I opted for a kiss for both of them on their cheeks as I cleared my plate and headed up to my room to study and finish the article Nate and I were working on regarding the service projects that the student government clubs were doing.

Felix had said that he'd call later. I hadn't ridden home with him since my birthday, and we needed to catch up. So, when my phone rang, I answered expecting it to be him. "Hey, Felix."

"It's Nate."

"Oh!" I pulled the phone from my ear to check the caller ID.

"Sorry to disappoint" he laughed.

"No, I just was expecting a call from Felix."

"I gathered."

"What's up?" I asked, hoping there wouldn't be an awkward lull in the conversation and still feeling slightly embarrassed from all the vulnerability in the supply closet.

"Just wanted to see where you were on our next piece. I heard that the student body president was doing something at the soup kitchen over on fourteenth if you wanted to go cover that together tomorrow?"

"I'm working on it now, actually."

"I'm sure you love how cutting-edge it is."

Was he really calling to check on the article, or was there something more?

"Do you need any help?" he asked. "You could come over, or we could meet somewhere?"

"Um, thanks. That's team player of you and all, but, after today, my parents are keeping an eagle's eye on me and probably wouldn't want me going anywhere."

"Oh…you told them about today?" he questioned with a twinge of concern on his voice.

"Yeah. I kinda tell them everything," I stated.

"Were they mad?" he asked after a long pause.

"At which part?" I laughed.

"Don't make me guess. Are they?"

"Well, Mom got pretty hung up on the supply closet with a boy scenario, and Dad was fired up over any parts that involved Ace."

"Ahh" was his only response, which was anticlimactic considering how worried he'd seemed about their reactions.

I changed the subject. "Did you hear anything new at practice?"

"Actually, yeah," he said.

"Why didn't you lead with that?" I laughed through my nose. "Way to bury the lead," I joked, not entirely sure he would get that reference.

"I wanted to see how you were doing. It wasn't all business."

"Oh," I said, softening back the sarcastic bristle. "Thanks. Sorry, proceed."

"Two guys were talking in the showers about a list. I couldn't hear the whole thing, but it sounds like there's a list about Mr. Hickham. That's all I could make out. I didn't want to seem like I was lurking in the showers."

"Hmmm," I said in a very British-detective sort of way, "a list, you say."

"A list," he repeated.

"A list of people, a list of names, a list of games won or lost, a list of money owed, a list of bodies buried with corresponding coordinates…"

"Bodies?"

"Too far?" I joked.

"A bit." He laughed.

Suddenly, I realized that we were getting along. Talking on the phone like friends. Were we friends? Frenemies? I didn't know, but something was starting to feel different...natural?

My phone beeped at me. It was Felix calling in. I didn't want to hang up on Nate, but I knew Felix wouldn't take no answer as an answer.

"Felix is calling. I gotta let you go."

"Oh. Oh, okay." He tried to mask the disappointment with nonchalance at the end. It didn't work.

"We're just friends, you know?" I felt the need to finally clarify that to him.

"You and Felix?" he asked in an obvious way.

"Yes."

"Okay."

"I do have to go. I'm sorry. I'll see you tomorrow. Thanks for calling."

"Sure. See ya."

I clicked over just at the last ring from Felix.

"Keeping me waiting, lady! What were you, in the bathroom again?" Felix harassed.

"No."

"What? It seems to be where you hang out these days."

"Gosh, Felix, like it's any of your business. And, if you must know, I was on the phone with Nate."

He perked right up. "Oh, do tell."

"He called to check on the article, but then, we just got to talking."

"Uh-huh. I spy with my nosy eye a *relationship*."

I brushed right past that. "I don't really think he called to talk about the article, because, come to think of it, we didn't really talk about it. I think he was just worried after what happened today."

"What. Happened. Today? And why didn't you call me on your way home if something happened? I've just been watching football with the Colonel all night, but I would have come over if I'd known there was something to be told."

I laughed and then recounted the whole story of the counselor, Ace, and the supply closet. Which, in and of itself, sounded like a game of CLUE. Nate, with the crutch, in the supply closet.

"I can't believe what you're telling me! Sylvie is getting blackmailed in two directions, and somehow Ace is involved in both. Nate and Sylvie did not have a baby together because they never had sex. Which thank god. And Mr. Hickham is still a bit of an unknown."

"That about covers it."

"And...you were in the supply closet with Nate Reinhart!" he exclaimed a little too loudly in my ear.

"Yes, but not like that. Don't make it sound so 'spin the bottle'."

"But the supply closet…" Felix teased.

"Stop it."

"Fine. So what, he's, like, helping you now?"

"Yeah. He's seeing what he can find out on the coach's end of things since we think we've figured out the Ace blackmail end of things. I really feel like it's all connected somehow."

"And you. What are you getting yourself into?"

"Nate told me to lay low. Keep my head down. Make Ace think he's gotten to me and I've dropped it."

"I like that guy. He says good things."

"Shut up."

"You know…," he said thoughtfully, "what I don't get is why Ace is threatening Sylvie to come forward but then threatening you to keep quiet and stop digging. If he wanted something exposed, shouldn't he be asking the reporter to help him?"

I leaned back in my chair and tossed my hair a bit. "That's a great point. Maybe he's not the one that wrote the note? But he did threaten me in the hall. He wants something to come out, but he's controlling it?"

"I do hear he does that."

"For a bunch of Christians, we sure do gossip a lot."

"Mmm-hmm."

"You going to the game on Friday?"

"Yep. Dinner first?"

"Yep. I'll tell Mom you're coming."

I wanted to hang up and text Nate about the idea I'd just had, but I needed finish the article, and I also wanted to call Carol. It was going to be a long night.

After another cup of coffee, I had finished the article and was about to email it to Nate when he texted me.

I JUST REMEMBERED SOMETHING ELSE.

WHAT IS IT?

I REMEMBERED THE GUYS SAYING THAT HE KEEPS THE LIST IN HIS DESK…

YOU'D MAKE A TERRIBLE SPY.

I KNOW.

SERIOUSLY WORST SPY EVER. BURIED THE LEAD.

I KNOW

I HAVE AN IDEA.

WHAT?

CAN YOU GET MY INTO THE LOCKER ROOM OR COACHES OFFICE DURING THE GAME?

TRICKY…

I KNOW

I'LL THINK OF SOMETHING

MAYBE I SHOULD. YOU'RE NOT A VERY GOOD SPY.

TRUE.

LET'S TALK TOMORROW.

K. REMEMBER. LOW KEY. HEAD DOWN.

YEP. OH! LAST THING. I JUST TALKED TO FELIX AND HE POINTED OUT THAT ACE WAS CONTROLLING EVERYTHING. HE WANTED TO EXPOSE SOMETHING; HE'S JUST MAKING SURE IT'S ON HIS TERMS AND SPUN THE RIGHT DIRECTION.

HE'S GOOD AT THAT. MAYBE WE CAN BEAT HIM TO IT AND MAKE SURE THE WHOLE TRUTH COMES OUT, NOT JUST HIS VERSION.

WE?

I'M A TERRIBLE SPY. YOU DID SAY YOU WANTED HELP.

I DO.

HENCE, THE WE…

ALSO. EMAILING YOU THE ARTICLE. LET ME KNOW WHAT YOU THINK. TOMORROW. I'M CRASHING IN TEN SECONDS.

9,8,7…NIGHT AVERY BRAVE

NIGHT.

7.

The next day, I was so low-key several teachers asked if I was there halfway through class even though they'd called roll. I ate lunch in the newspaper room with Mr. Knight and Felix, then left campus early to cover the soup kitchen with Nate, who ended up not being able to show because practice ran late. I thought that was odd considering he was on crutches, but he texted me later.

I DIDN'T EVEN SEE YOU TODAY. WHERE YA BEEN?

HEAD DOWN, REMEMBER?

OH. YOU'RE GOOD.

SORRY TO BAIL ON THE SOUP KITCHEN.

NOT MAD. IT WAS SOUP.

NOT SALAD?

OR BREADSTICKS.

☺

The next day was Friday. I tried to be as low-key as the day before, though I felt like I was so good at it that it was drawing more attention to me than usual. But in keyboarding class, Nate kept looking at me around his computer, and he wouldn't stop. Finally, I nodded for him to change computers since I was in the back row. He made up an excuse to the teacher about how his crutches were in the way and his ankle was aching and he needed room to stretch it out and came over to the only other vacant computer by me. I leaned down in front of my screen, hidden from the teacher. He did the same, though he was so tall that it didn't really work, so he slouched down in his chair low enough that he was finally hidden.

"What? Why were you staring at me?"

"I wasn't staring!" he whispered defensively.

"Okay. Not staring. But you kept looking at me."

"I think I have a way in tonight. But we'd have to time it perfectly."

"Okay."

"Meet me outside the field house after school. I'll explain it then."

"Don't you think it's better if we're not seen together near the field house just before I break into it?"

"You're not breaking in. But good point. Can you give me a ride home after school? That would give us a chance to plan. Alone."

The way he said *alone* made my spine tingle. "Sure," I managed to whisper, though my tongue was dry and heavy. The days when I'd thought he couldn't stand me had been easier to navigate than whatever just happened. *Nothing happened, Avery. Get over it,* I scolded myself.

"Okay. I'll meet you out front."

My stomach twisted with anxiety as the bell rang and I gathered my books. *Can I prolong this by going to my locker first? Maybe he will think I left without him? Why am I so nervous to drive Nate home?* It wasn't like we'd never been alone before in a dark classroom against the wall, I scolded myself, and in a supply closet. *You're being childish Avery Brave!*

I skipped my locker and walked toward the front of the school only to be met by the pretentious Mr. Hickham. He stood in the center of the lobby with his whistle and badge, clearly trying to stand his ground or mark his territory.

"Ahhh, Ms. Nightingale."

"Hello, Mr. Hickham." I reminded myself to stay calm. I hadn't done anything wrong and, as of yet, I hadn't accused him of anything.

"How's the paper going? Got any nail-biting exposés coming up?" I could see him trying not to smirk, but it unfurled at the corners of his mouth as he mocked me with his words.

"Yes, sir." I nodded, trying to think of a way out.

"And hopefully you'll write an exciting victory story about tonight's game?"

"I wouldn't miss it, sir." I mustered a smile and excused myself out the front of the building where I finally let the shiver I'd held back run down my spine.

Nate was posted up by the Saints sign with his crutches leaning beside him. *Here we go,* I thought as I walked over to him.

"When do you get to get off those things?"

"Hey," he said, getting off his phone and shoving it in his back pocket as he reached for his crutches. "Next week, I go back in to get my cast off I think, but I'll still have to have a boot or something and probably can't put weight on it for a little bit. But I think I can drive maybe next week."

"Oh. That's good."

"Yep. Ready to go?"

"Sure."

The ride to his house was shorter than expected and less awkward than I had envisioned. He told it all, planned out and timed to the minute during the opening song as the team and the coaches ran out on the field. I'd have a small window, and it would be a risk for no one to see me go in or come out, but it was my only chance to see what was on that list.

"You're actually wearing school colors!" Felix exclaimed in an accusatory voice as we walked into the stadium.

I looked down. I thought I had been subtle about it, but apparently not. My red skinny ankle jeans that were rolled at the bottom and my Navy tank top were a little too close to our school colors for Felix's taste, but at least I didn't wear my school spirit shirt, which I almost had but decided against considering I was about to perform a covert mission in the assistant coach's office. I felt like that would've been in bad taste.

"And you have makeup on. What's happening? What's going on?"

"Nothing!" I scolded him. "Can't I wear real clothes and makeup without getting undermined by you?"

He gave me a suspicious look as we sat down next to my

parents in the stands. I pensively watched the field as the cheerleaders lined up next to the enormous blowup cloud tunnel that the team and coaches ran through. The fake smoke began to billow out from behind it. That was my queue to start heading down the stands to the field house.

Just as I was about to stand up, Ace ran through the tunnel holding a hand-painted sign that read, THE QUEEN IS DEAD.

I looked around to see if anyone had seen it, and ripples of gasps rolled through the crowd, but my parents seemed to be oblivious.

Well played, Ace. But you have no idea what's coming. I stood up, held my head high, because I knew people were watching, and kept to the mission.

"I'm going to go get a soda. You guys want something? Felix—popcorn?"

"Nah. I'm good. Hurry back. You love the part where they burst through the clouds to 'when the saints go marching in'," he joked.

Mom and Dad both shook their heads, and I headed down the steps but only made it down three before Felix caught my arm.

"What?" I said. "Did you change your mind?"

He leaned low and whispered, "Are you rendezvousing with Nate? Did you see that sign? Maybe you are not laying as low as you think," he talked quickly.

"No!" I wriggled free from his hand and slapped it jokingly. "And nobody says 'rendezvous'." Now, I was behind. I had to hurry.

"I say it," he retorted as I hurried away from him, "and that's all you need to know."

Once I was down the stairs, I jogged a few steps to hopefully make up the time I'd lost with Felix. I heard the band warming up in the stands, and, ahead, the team jogged out of the field house and gathered at the entrance of the cloud tunnel. I caught Nate's eye at the back of the mass of helmets, and he quickly looked down. Just as the band began to play and the team began to chant, I got a text from him.

NOW

The music bellowed across the stadium, and the team, unified and fired up, chanted like an army. I could hear people beginning to sing the words to the song until the team began to run through the tunnel, and then the stands erupted in cheers and hollers.

I walked backwards for a few steps, pretending to cheer with everyone and counting coaches and players, like Nate had told me to. Everyone was out. I slipped in the side door of the field house. The pungent locker room smell made me take a step back, but I recovered by pulling my shirt up over my nose. I had a minute and a half before someone was bound to come back in, whether it was a water boy or a defensive coordinator or a referee. They might not…but they might.

I ran to the desk Nate had told me was Assistant Coach Hickham's. The top of the desk was a mess, covered in papers and whiteboards with plays written on them. If the list was as secretive as the players said, it wouldn't just be sitting out on the top for anyone to find. I check the drawers. The drawers didn't match the top. The methodical and organized placement of pens, notepads, and name tags suggested that Mr. Hickham was not the same person underneath as he appeared to be on the outside. But I was reading too much into it. There was no list.

The handle jiggled. I jumped and hid under the desk. The footsteps were light and quick, a younger kid—the ball boy or the water boy, probably. He paused in front of the desk I was under, and that was when I saw it! A folded piece of paper was taped underneath the desk in the back right-hand corner. It would have been hidden under the drawer, but I had pulled the drawer out! The boy picked up something off the floor and turned back toward the door. As he left, he turned the lights off. I grabbed my phone and shined it up toward the paper. I didn't want to take it, because, if Hickham came looking for it, he'd know someone was onto him. But, if I could get the information without taking it, he'd be blindsided when a picture of it showed up in the front page of the newspaper.

I snapped several photos with my phone and carefully slipped out the door and wove my way through the concession stand line.

"Avery?"

I spun around to see Sylvie in my face. "Oh, hey, Sylvie. Did I step on your foot? I'm sorry." I hoped she wouldn't notice that I had just cut in front of her to try to blend in.

"I didn't see you there," she sneered.

"Here I am." I shrugged, trying to play it off. "Shouldn't you guys be out there, you know, cheering?" I asked snarkily.

"Not that it's any of your business, but, as you can see, the whole squad isn't here; just us three. Coach told us we could have a break while the rest did some fly cheers. We just needed a snack."

I nodded, only half listening and trying to keep an eye on Nate and the locker room door.

"So…what, are the King and Queen together now?" Sylvie blurted out abrasively. Whitney and Brooklynn giggled behind her.

"No! We're not together. We just have to work on the paper together."

"Oh." She started to twirl her high ponytail that had a navy bow the size of Texas perched on top. "Ace said you guys were together now," she said matter-of-factly as if it would ruffle me to hear that.

"Well," I said stepping up to the counter, pausing to order my soda, taking it, and turning back to her, "Ace says a lot of things that aren't true." I winked at her and walked off, not letting it show how fast my heart was beating. I texted Nate as I walked back to the stands

GOT IT.

In the second half, raindrops began to fall from above the stadium lights. Everyone got out their umbrellas, and we tried to stick it out, because, so far, there was no lightening. I caught Nate's eye once when he turned around to look up in the stands.

It did something strange to my stomach to see him standing there in the rain, in his jersey, looking at me.

Felix scooted closer to share my umbrella. "What's going on?"

"It's raining, and we're winning."

"Not that. That," he said, nodding toward Nate with his chin.

"Nothing."

"It can't be nothing, because it's definitely something." He scooted even closer and whispered in my hair. "Either a) you're up to something or b) you just rendezvoused to make out behind the bleachers."

I elbowed him in the ribs, "a) Nobody says rendezvous because it implies a tryst or something sketchy and b) I can't tell you. I need you to be innocent by admission. And c) did you see him leave the field? No."

"I don't think you did that right."

"Which part?" I sassed.

He squinted at me and tilted his chin up. "Probably all of it. But definitely B."

"You know what I mean. If I tell you, then you'll be guilty because you knew."

"Are you guilty because you know?"

"No. Because I'm going to do right thing with *what* I know."

"Is this a revenge story on a certain person that has a name that trumps most any other card in a deck?"

"No," I insisted. "I don't do revenge stories. I do truth."

He pretended to drop the mic, and I shook my head.

We tried to stay longer, but the rain kept falling harder, and my jeans were sticking to me, they were so wet. And with one large strike of lightening that lit up the entire sky, they called off the game.

We took Felix home, and, as we drove back to our house, my parents asked me about Nate, my safety, Felix, and the mystery I was trying to solve. I talked to them transparently, all the while feeling like my phone was burning a hole in my back pocket. I wanted to see what was on the list, but I hadn't looked yet for fear that someone else would see it.

I excused myself to go change while Mom said she was going to get snacks ready for the movie we were going to watch. I raced upstairs to my room and closed the door. I stripped out of my wet clothes and hung them to dry in the bathroom. Wrapped in my robe and wadding my hair up on top of my head in a messy, curly bun, I ran over to my bed where my phone was vibrating. It was Nate.

I NEED TO SEE YOU

My stomach did a somersault, and I felt like I needed to sit down. *Don't read anything into it, Avery*

Brave, I reprimanded myself.

NOW?

CAN YOU?

I'M SUPPOSED TO WATCH A MOVIE WITH MY PARENTS.

CAN YOU TELL THEM YOU'RE GOING TO BED? THEN COME MEET ME?

THAT SOUNDS SKETCH. AND I DON'T LIE TO MY PARENTS. OR SNEAK OUT. I'LL GO ASK THEM AND SEE IF IT'S OKAY FOR YOU TO COME OVER. I WAS JUST ABOUT TO TEXT YOU THE PICTURES OF THE LIST.

NO! DON'T. I DON'T WANT THEM ON MY PHONE. TOO RISKY. I WANT TO SEE IT PERSON.

OK. HOLD ON.

I ran down the steps to find my dad already half asleep in his recliner. "Dad?"

"Yeah?" he said, sitting up at the sight of me next to him. "What's up, Avery?"

"Since the game got cancelled, Nate wants to work on the article we have due for Monday. Is that okay?"

"Sure, sweetie. Do you want to invite him over here?"

"Would you like me to?"

"Would you like me to like you to? You seem hesitant."

"I am hesitant, though I don't know why. So maybe it would feel safer to have him come here. If that's okay with you and Mom. We can just work in the kitchen?"

"Wise choice, hon. Thanks for being honest and safe."

I kissed the top of his head and jogged back upstairs to my phone. I decided to call instead of texting, because my stomach continued to do flops at the words "I need to see you" on my phone.

"Hey. They said it's fine. But…" I paused, suddenly realizing he might not want to come here. What if he really did want to rendezvous? But the thought of Felix saying that repeatedly made my smile and forget that thought altogether. "They would prefer it if you'd come here? Is that okay?"

"Oh. Um—" He paused, and I worried again that he had another agenda. "That's cool." He finished rather cryptically, "I was going to say the village inn has free pie after 10 p.m. But it's fine. I can come there."

"I do love pie…," I joked, "but we can just work in the kitchen here if that's okay."

"Sure. Give me twenty."

"Okay."

I decided that, since this was not a rendezvous, I didn't need to look good. And, also if I didn't, maybe it would deter any ulterior motives.

Throwing on some sweatpants and a t-shirt, I jogged downstairs to make some coffee. The doorbell rang just as the coffee finished brewing. My parents had already started watching their movie, so I called out toward the theater room, "I'll get it."

I opened the door to Nate, who had a hat on, no doubt to shield himself from the still-blooming thunderstorm. *He looks good in a hat*, I thought. He also held a to-go box.

"Did you bring leftovers?" I teased as I opened the door wider to let him in.

"No. I brought pie."

I felt in my brow lift my mouth into a smile, must have been infectious, because he smiled too.

"You said you loved pie."

"I did. I mean, I do."

"Okay." He shrugged and set the pie down on the table,

sliding down in a chair.

I suddenly felt ridiculous for my sweatpants and wet hair, but the way he was looking at me led me to believe that he hadn't even noticed them yet. Feeling my face grow pink from his stare, I turned and walked toward the coffee station. "Want some coffee to go with the pie?"

"Yes, ma'am. Please."

I poured two cups, taking as long as I could so that I could leave my back to him as long as possible. When I couldn't stir the coffee any more, I returned to the table.

"So…did you look at the list yet?" he asked, and I shushed him. "Sorry. I thought your parents knew already. You said you—"

"I do. I just haven't told them this yet."

"They didn't know you went to the field house tonight?"

I shook my head as I took a sip of coffee. "Felix either," I added.

I dished out the two slices of chocolate pie and then opened my laptop and set my phone between us. I opened the photo of the list. It included practically half the football team and most of the cheer squad along with several student government leaders. Nate leaned back in his chair as if what he'd just seen was heavy. He sighed and rubbed his face.

I stated the obvious. "You're not on there."

"No. I'm not. Did you think I would be?"

"No, but if you were, it might give us a clue as to what it's for."

"True. Let's look at who is on there and see if there are any common factors."

I began typing as we both threw out hypothetical scenarios that might cause Hickham to make a list of students. They ranged from simple to deranged, but even still, they all seem implausible.

By the time we wound down, we'd drained the entire pot of coffee and ate all the pie, and my parents had retired to bed. The storm still rumbled outside, and the sound of the rain on the windows and the roof was lulling me into exhaustion. I spread out my arm on the table and laid my head on it.

"You're tired. I should go. My mom has been texting me about where I am for about thirty minutes," Nate said, checking his phone again. And then, his face lit up like he'd gotten shocked. He reached across the table and touched my arm; it felt like the lightening had come through the house. "That's it."

"What is?" I said, sitting up so fast I got dizzy. "What is it?"

"The phones."

"What phones?"

"Sylvie lost her phone at the end of last year. About a month later, so did Ace. I've seen several players get their phones confiscated while we watched film a class, but I always just assumed it was because they got caught texting instead of watching."

He stood up and started to pace as best he could on crutches around the kitchen.

"It's not a complete theory, but what if these are all the phones that Mr. Hickham has, and they all have something in common? What if Hickham is blackmailing these students somehow with their phones?"

I typed it all out on the screen and read it back to myself. Nate leaned over me and read my screen. He was right above me, leaning on the table with one hand. I could smell the rain on him mixed with his cologne. I felt like, if I moved at all, we'd touch faces. I flashed back to the dance, and my face grew red—I hoped he couldn't see.

"Well, aside from the idea that it's just a list of confiscated phones, and in light of what I've heard Sylvie say *and* the fact that it was taped underneath his desk…it's the most plausible thing we've come up with so far. How can we figure out if the rest of the people on the list 'lost' their phones or got them taken away?"

"Maybe one of them will talk?"

"I doubt it if they're being blackmailed by Hickham."

"What do you think he's making them do?"

"I'm too tired to go there. It's probably the stuff of nightmares."

"Yeah, better not. Sorry I stayed so late."

I yawned while trying to say, "No, it's fine."

"Well, thanks. Tell your parents I said thanks."

"I will. Thanks for the pie."

He shrugged again just like he had when he'd brought it in. "You said you loved pie."

"I know, but I also love daises and horses. Are you going to buy me those too?" I said sarcastically.

"Maybe," he answered teasingly.

"Well, not tonight," I said, opening the door and walking out onto the front porch with him. It was still storming, and I jumped a little when the thunder crashed right above us. As he walked past me, Nate brushed my hand with his, and I could have sworn he did it on purpose.

"Not tonight," he echoed, and it sounded like a promise. I was so tired that, as he jogged in the rain to his car, I leaned up against the large white pillar on the edge of the porch and let my head rest against it. I closed my eyes and listened to the rain fall all around the house. His lights flickered at me, and he drove off.

Nate was quite possibly the most confusing, surprising, and sometimes infuriating boy I knew. But tonight, he'd brought me pie. And that was something. We used to hate each other or, at best, steer clear of each other, but something was definitely changing.

8.

"What do you mean, Felix?" I demanded, feeling very defensive.

"I mean that he's thinking about sending me away to have tests run," Felix repeated, folding his arms and leaning against the locker next to mine.

"You don't have a disease, Felix." I said flatly. "What does he expect them to find?"

He hung his head and studied the red pattern on the floor that we jokingly referred as the red brick road. "I think he just wants to find a reason why I'm not 'normal'. And possibly a remedy. A medication."

I slammed my locker and grabbed both of his arms. "Look at me, Felix."

He wouldn't.

"Felix! Look at me."

Reluctantly, he looked up from the floor to find my eyes filled with tears just like his. "There's nothing wrong with you. Okay?!"

His tears spilled over and tripped over his cheeks.

"Say 'okay'."

He shook his head.

"Say 'okay', Felix."

"I can't."

"Why not?"

"Because, Avery, I have a military father, I go to a private Christian school, and we live in the south. Being Felix isn't okay."

"Even if you've started to believe them, even if you don't feel okay, *you're okay*. Do you hear me?"

He nodded finally and wiped his face with his sleeve. The bell rang, but neither of us moved.

"Would it help if I pretended to be your girlfriend?"

A slight smile hooked the corner of Felix's mouth but quickly disappeared. "No. I've always been this way. I've never been what they wanted me to be, and not just when it comes to girls. It's not like I grew up weird. I like the military and guns, football, wrestling, hockey, fast cars...heck, I'd even drink beer if the colonel would let me. I've just never cared about dating. But it means a lot to me that you would do that for me."

"Felix, I'm pretty sure I would do anything for you. You're the best friend I have."

I wasn't just saying it to help him feel better. Carol was my longest friend—we'd been friends since grade school—but Felix and I had something different.

"Thanks, Avery Brave."

I took his arms, and we started down the hallway. When we rounded the corner down the east hallway, a determined Mr. Hickham was coming our way. Felix didn't know what I'd done or discovered, but I squeezed his arm anyway, hoping that he'd know it meant, *"Don't leave me."*

As Mr. Hickham approached, his face was set in a grimace, and he was coming for me. Felix shot a look down at me that said, *"What have you done?"*

"Ms. Nightingale. Might I have a word?" Mr. Hickham said diplomatically but with anger behind it.

"Sure, Mr. Hickham. What can I do for you?" I said, pretending not to know what this was about.

"Maybe I speak to you privately in my office, please?"

"This is Felix. Anything you need to ask, you can ask in front of Felix."

"Nice to meet you, Felix. You're a new student, aren't you?"

"Yes, sir." Felix answered with a nod.

"Well, as a new student, you may not know that, if an administrator asks to speak with you, then you need to comply." He spoke to Felix though obviously reprimanding me.

"Good to know, sir," Felix said awkwardly.

"I can always send a written sequester if it needs to come to that, Ms. Nightingale."

"Maybe that would be best, sir." *Always leave a paper trail*, I thought.

"As the assistant principal, I'm disappointed in your uncooperativeness and stubbornness. These are definitely not attributes of truly great Saints."

"With all due respect, sir, you're the principal's assistant, not the assistant principal. And while I don't enjoy contradicting you, the Saints of old stood for justice, truth, and those who couldn't speak for themselves. Which often appeared to those in authority as being stubborn and insubordinate. That's why they were stoned, beheaded, and crucified," I finished proudly, though I knew that I most likely would get detention for this.

Mr. Hickham moved to speak but was so flustered that he just huffed loudly and marched up to the front office, no doubt to tell the principal what I'd just said. Felix stared at me, stunned.

"What?"

"You're insane."

"Well, someone needed to say it."

"Have fun in detention. Want me to tell your parents you're with me?"

"No!" I insisted. "I don't lie to me parents, Felix."

"Okay, well, I'll see you in a few weeks."

"Why do you say that?"

"You'll be grounded for sure! Sometimes, I can't believe you actually say the things you say out loud."

"Whatever. After everything that is about to come out about Hickham…my parents won't even care about what I said. My dad will probably be proud."

Felix stopped mid-stride in the center of the hallway. It was clear we were not going to make it to class, and we'd probably get detention for that as well. *Oh well, add it to the tab.*

"What's about to go down? Is this about what happened at the game?"

"I don't want to tell you. I don't want you to get in trouble because of what you know."

"I think I'm glad you're trying to protect me, but who's going to protect you? Seems like you're getting in over your head, Avery."

"Everything is fine. We just need a little more proof, and then we can take this upward."

"'We'?!"

"Nate and I."

"Wait. What?"

"He's been helping me."

"You guys are a rollercoaster."

"My dad said it was about squid pro quo."

"You *definitely* didn't do that right, and I have no idea what you were trying to say."

But before I could answer, Sylvie came running toward me in her uniform. They had a pep rally today and an away game tonight. But she didn't look peppy; she looked distraught.

"Avery—we need to talk."

Felix unhooked our arms and told me he'd see me later. I gave him a pleading look, and he just shrugged with a smirk on his face. *Traitor.*

"What do you want, Sylvie?" I asked sternly.

"Can we go somewhere and talk? Alone."

Why does everyone need to talk to me alone today?

I looked around. Where did she expect us to go? This was a high school. And then I saw it, just down the hall. *The supply closet.* I laughed.

"Please, step into my office," I said, leading the way.

"Where are we…" She trailed off as I opened the door. "Seriously, Avery?"

"Seriously. Now get in."

I closed the door and locked it behind us.

"I heard you've seen the list."

What? My head spun. The only person who knew I'd seen it was Nate. Would he tell Sylvie? Would he betray me? He brought me pie; didn't that mean something? Or maybe it was a distraction. Maybe it was to gain my trust and then out me. I boiled inside, but I studied Sylvie carefully. *What if she's trying to test me? What if she's trying to get me to give up the list? What if she doesn't know anything?*

"What list?" I thought fast. "Oh! You mean the Who's Who list? Yeah, I'm afraid, Sylvie…you're not on it this year. So sorry."

"Stop it, Avery. You know what I'm talking about. Hickham's list."

Nate had told her. I clenched my fist so that my face wouldn't react. But something in my chest ached and felt heavy like it was caving in.

"I don't know what you're talking about, Sylvie."

She stepped closer to me, and I tripped backward over a bucket, landing on the floor. She didn't even flinch. Her blue eyes narrowed, and her mouth puckered in sour anger. "You listen here, Avery Nightingale. You have no idea what you're getting into. You could ruin everything if you're not careful."

She looked as though she might hit me, she was so angry. Her lip was quivering, and her hands were shaking as she raised them. I decided in that moment it was worth the risk to level with her.

"Sylvie—stop."

She backed up, and I scrambled to my feet. "What if I knew that it's not just Hickham who had you under his thumb but Ace too?"

Her eyes grew wide and confirmed what I'd thought.

"What if I knew that they both have something on you that could get you kicked out of Saints but also ruin your chance at getting into any of your colleges of choice?"

Tears started streaming down Sylvie's cheeks, dragging mascara with them. She hung her head. "Then you know more than I thought you did."

"What does Hickham have on you?"

She blinked up at me. "I thought you knew."

"I don't know what it is, but I know he has some tight stranglehold on you. And others. What is it?"

"I can't tell you."

"But Sylvie, you're letting both of them control you. Wouldn't you rather turn the tables and control your own future?"

"That's easier said than done. You don't know what we've done."

"Not the way I see it. All I need is proof, and I can write a story, take it to the authorities, and expose whatever Hickham is doing—and, as a bonus, take Ace down with him."

"Ace never goes down. You know that better than anyone. He'll always get away with whatever he does."

I bit back the sting of bitterness and tears. I choked on my fear. She knew what had happened last year. And yet she was so afraid of Ace that she wouldn't come forward about that or what he made her do this year or even whatever it was that Hickham was doing to all of them. It made my cheeks burn and my heart beat fast, and my own words echoed in my ears: *The Saints of old stood for justice, truth, and those who couldn't speak for themselves.*

"Sylvie, I decided recently to be done feeling powerless. I'm done being scared of Ace. Which, in a way, is also scary. So, when you're ready to stop being under everyone's thumb, let me know. Ace might get away with it, but that doesn't mean we can't tell the truth. What we do with the truth matters."

I pushed past her and left the supply closet. The bell rang, and the hallway filled with kids streaming from one class to another. I felt as though I was moving with the crowd in slow motion. I felt alone in a hallway full of kids. *Maybe I was right in the beginning. Maybe I knew exactly who Nate Reinhart was.*

He was Ace's friend. Someone who pretend to be trustworthy just to…*what, Avery? Get close to me? Is that what he was trying to do?*

It didn't matter. He was someone who would tell Sylvie that I'd seen the list. I didn't know how to trust anyone. Maybe *I* was the terrible spy, second-guessing myself at every turn. What was the saying, trust no one and validate later? No—I was doing that wrong. Maybe it was never trust, and always verify. *That one applies, but I still don't think I'm doing it right.* Either way—I wasn't sure who to trust.

I slid into my seat in the newspaper room and didn't even look in Nate's direction. My eyes burned as I fought back the tears and the anger that bubbled in my stomach. Mr. Knight's eyes were boring into me from behind his desk. He could tell something was wrong, but if he asked, I was certain that I would just burst into tears and run out of the room.

All of this control was causing me to sweat and get hot. I couldn't take it; I couldn't sit it the same room as Nate. I wanted to yell at him. But, thankfully, the door opened, and an office assistant came in and handed Mr. Knight a note. He looked at me and motioned for me to come up to his desk.

It was my paper trail. Hickham was summoning me to his office. I could feel Nate's eyes on me, and I wanted to glare at him so badly, but I knew it would hurt just to look at him even if my look also hurt him.

I took the note from Mr. Knight. He asked me quietly if I was okay. I nodded and slipped out of the room. Before I reached the office, I set my phone to record and slipped it into my jacket pocket. As I knocked on Mr. Hickham's door, he called in a flat tone for me to come in. He told me to sit down and walked behind me to shut the door.

"Do you know what this is about, Avery?"

"My name is Avery Brave. And no, sir."

He pursed his lips at my correction and folded his hands on top of his desk.

"Ms. Nightingale," he started, "I've heard some rumors that I'd like to address, because they are particularly worrisome."

"Rumors?" I played along innocently.

"Have you not heard them?"

"No, sir."

"Can this possibly mean that you are the one who has been starting them, then?"

"No, sir. I don't start rumors. I tell the truth."

"So, you're implying that the rumors are true."

"No, sir. I don't even know what rumors you're referring to."

"I think you do, Ms. Nightingale."

I leaned forward. "With all due respect, again, sir—I don't. I suppose you could tell me what the rumors are, and I could tell you if they are true or not."

Mr. Hickham pounded his fist on the desk. "Don't play games with me, Avery."

"It's 'Avery Brave'."

"Rumors like this can get someone fired," he sneered at me in a low voice, "or get someone in a lot of trouble." He narrowed his eyes.

"Mr. Hickham, are you threatening me in some way?"

"I can see that you enjoy chasing drama," he said, jabbing me cryptically with his words. "I am warning you. If you have anything to do with these rumors going around, or if you are snooping in the wrong place…you could get yourself in a whole heap of trouble."

"Well, I can assure you, Mr. Hickham, I am a reporter, so I investigate and report, but I never snoop."

"I'm serious, Avery."

"My name is Avery Brave. And so am I."

I stood and walked out of his office, hiding my trembling hands in my jacket pockets where I turned the recording off. I slipped into the bathrooms and hid in the last stall and cried until the bell rang. I wiped my eyes and tried to breathe deeply to clear away the blotches that covered my face and neck when I cried. I was just about to leave to go back to Mr. Knight's class to get my bag when two girls entered, talking.

"All I know is that's the dumbest mistake in history."

"I know."

"I mean, come on, you don't look at that kind of stuff during class. How dumb are they? You'll get yourself on the list for that kind of stuff."

The list? What kind of stuff?

"How do they get away with that stuff anyway? I know my mom would totally find out. She's like a ninja or something."

"Mine too."

Soon, they changed the subject and left without giving any other details. As I walked to Mr. Knight's class, I tried to put the clues together. *They all got their cellphones taken away by Mr. Hickham, and he's made a list of everyone whose phone he's taken. They are all under his thumb. But why? Or how? And what's he making them do?*

But my thoughts were cut short by the sound of Nate's crutches coming out of Mr. Knight's class. I fell back and stood behind the corner that was just before the door so he wouldn't see me. I heard him crutch away from me down the hall, and I sighed.

Entering Mr. Knight's class, I saw that Mr. Knight had already left for the day. Nate must have been waiting around for me. I didn't care; I didn't want to talk to him. But I knew that it was time to talk to my parents. This was getting deep, and I knew that they deserved to know what I was getting into.

As I walked to my car, I heard my name faintly behind me. But I didn't turn to see who it was. I was done talking for the day. The voice called again, louder this time, and I could tell now that it was Nate. He was slow enough on his crutches that I knew I could get in my car and drive away before he reached the parking lot. Which was a horrid thing to do, but it was what I was doing.

I couldn't hear him calling after me anymore once I shut the door, but I could see him going as fast as he could on his crutches to try to catch me in my rearview mirror. My heart felt sad as I drove away, feeling the loss of whatever I had thought was happening between us. I had obviously been wrong.

9.

"I love your spirit, Avery Brave. I love your tenacity," Dad said, sipping his coffee and crossing his legs. "But this is an awfully nasty accusation that you're talking about."

Mother nodded her head and looked worriedly at me. They hadn't gotten upset when I'd told them about the field house or what I'd said to Mr. Hickham. But they were concerned about the accusation I was making. And rightly so.

"I know that we've had a lot of accusation come from our house in the past year or so, and that didn't go in our favor, but don't you think that we should care about what is potentially happening to these students more than we care about how it looks to make the accusation?"

Father reached for my hand, and I held it across the table. I knew he wanted me to be safe and find some sense of normal after last year, but I couldn't just sit back and un-see what I'd come across or un-know what I'd uncovered.

"Well, promise you'll come to us first before you publish, okay?"

"Okay."

"And I'm sorry that you feel betrayed by this Nate. He seemed like a good kid."

"I don't *feel* betrayed, Mom. I have *been* betrayed. No one else knew! He had to have told Sylvie." I raised my voice more than I intended. "Sorry. I didn't mean to yell."

"It's okay, dear. But you need to forgive him. I don't want any of this to be about revenge. On any of them. You made a very good point about the saints of old. Stand up for justice. Speak out for those who feel they can't. But don't seek revenge on people just because they sin. They need forgiveness and grace just as much as you or I do. God administers justice, not us."

"I know, Mom." Her words struck a chord in my heart—a painful and haunting minor chord. "But what's that quote about evil prospering because good people do nothing?"

"Edmund Burke said that," Dad confirmed, "and you're right. You can't do nothing. And we're not suggesting that you do nothing. But we just want you to be safe in whatever it is you feel you have to do."

I nodded.

Dad sat back, dismissing the matter for the night. "Remember, we have the meeting at church tonight, but we'll be home around ten. Okay?"

I nodded, glad I would have some quiet time alone after the day I'd just had. I told them I'd clean up the kitchen for them so they could go. They both hugged me and kissed my head as they left.

I finished my work from the class that Felix and I had skipped this morning and I worked on my article about the auditions for the play the theater class was doing this fall.

I called Carol, but she was busy with homework. I decided to call Felix.

"Want me to come over? You sound sad."

"Do I?" I asked back, settling into one of the chairs in our home theater. "I'm okay. I'm just going to watch a movie, I think. My folks are gone, so it's nice to be alone for a while."

"You sure?"

"Yeah."

"Avery Brave?"

"Yeah?"

"You know you can tell me what happened with Ace. Anytime you're ready. You can trust me."

I hesitated and felt my mouth open as if I was going to tell him. My heart did ache to tell him the truth. But then, the phone beeped; someone was calling. "I know," I said. "Thanks, Felix. I've got another call. I'd better go."

"Okay," Felix said reluctantly. "Call me later if you want."

"Okay, bye."

I hung up and saw that it was Nate calling. I paused before answering, wondering if I should talk to him. Then, I slid the "accept" button and answered. "Hello?"

"Avery?"

"My name is Avery Brave," I said in the same tone that I'd used with Mr. Hickham.

"What's the matter?"

I didn't answer. I felt the anger bubble up again.

"Avery Brave? You there?"

"I'm here. I thought you'd be at the away game."

"I am."

He was calling me from the game? No—I wasn't going to fall for this again.

"Oh. Well…just send me your notes for the article, and I'll edit them tomorrow."

"Avery Brave—I didn't call about the article. What's going on? You didn't seem like yourself in class."

"I really don't want to talk, Nate."

"At all or to me?"

"Either."

He paused, and it was awkwardly silent on the phone.

"Are you mad at me? What did I do?" He sounded hurt and sincere. But maybe this was just another ploy to get under my skin.

"You know what you did."

"Avery Brave, please talk to me. I have no idea what you're mad about."

Losing my temper, I stomped my foot and yelled into the phone, "You told Sylvie!"

"Told Sylvie what? I didn't tell her anything."

"She cornered me today, and she knew that I knew about the list. You're the only one who knew about the field house. You told her!"

"Avery—listen to me. I did not tell Sylvie anything. I don't speak to Sylvie, pretty much as a general rule, ever."

"Then how did she know?" I demanded.

"I have no idea."

I heard someone enter the room he was in and say something to him.

"I gotta go. Call you later."

"Please don't," I said shortly and hung up. Huffing heavily, I threw the phone across the room. But within minutes, I picked it back up and called Felix.

"Wanna come over?"

"Be right there."

I met him on the front porch. He hugged me before either of us spoke. With my head buried in his shirt, I mumbled, "I didn't know who else to call. And I realized you were my best friend. And best friends tell each other everything. So, I'm ready if you're ready."

Felix pulled me over to the porch swing, and we sat together. His face was pensive except for his big brown compassionate eyes.

"My dad said once that, if Ace is willing to act the way he does in public, then he knew good and well that he's capable of much worse in private."

I took a deep breath, then dove into my story.

"We dated for a year, almost two. I was a very different girl when we started. I was shy and soft, and, after the fact, we could all see that Ace preyed on that. At first, he was commanding but in a sort of assertive way. He's big, strong, and decisive. Our relationship was that way too. I, the shy one, let him, the decisive and loud one, boss me around and command our every move.

"But about eight months in, he started getting angry when I would disagree. And I found that I actually disagreed with him a lot. And one night, we were kissing, regrettably, and he wanted to go further. I told him no. And I told him that, if he didn't stop pushing, I was leaving. Well, nobody stands up to Ace without getting put back in their place. That was the first night he hit me."

Felix's mouth fell open. I met his eyes and raised a hand. *There's more.*

"He slapped me the first time, open palm. It didn't bruise, and no one ever knew. But it hurt so bad. I cried about it every time I looked in the mirror. I began to excuse it, because, if I didn't, I would have to face the shame of having allowed it, I supposed.

"This continued. For months. He was a rollercoaster, and it was nauseating to keep up. But my fear was building, and I felt like I couldn't get out. I quit talking to my parents, and I made excuses for the bruises at home and at school.

"He made me feel like it was my fault. And yet he had such a hold on me emotionally that he wouldn't let me go, and I couldn't get out. I was stuck in this cycle of love, lust, anger, pain, and forgiveness. And it sickens me now that I was so entrapped. But it's true.

"The last night he hit me, I had gone to his house to surprise him. It was his birthday. He'd pressured me for so long that I was actually considering, you know...for his birthday. I can't believe—well. Never mind.

"I walked in on him, and...what I didn't know at the time was that he was with Sylvie. But because I caught him, he got angry. More like enraged. Because, you know, it was my fault for coming over unnoticed and not his fault for cheating on me..."

I rolled my eyes and took a breath, giving Felix time to react if he wanted since he'd sat there so pensively stoic the entire time, but he didn't. So, I continued on.

"Sylvie hid under the covers like a little coward and let him hit me repeatedly. I tried to block him, but he just started to kick me instead. Finally, I escaped out the door, but he caught me at the top of the stairs. He pushed me down two flights of stairs. I landed at the bottom with two broken ribs, a broken arm, and a fractured ankle. My face was black and blue as well as my back.

"When I came to, his parents were standing at the bottom of the stairs, speechless and unmoving. Instead of rushing to my aid, they rushed to his. I called the police and my parents from the floor. I've never felt so alone, in so much pain, or so helpless in my whole life.

"My parents and I were rushed to the hospital, and I assumed the police would be right behind us with Ace in custody. But they never came. They, his parents, blamed it on me. The used their power, money, and influence to get Ace out of any charges. We pressed charges and hired a really good lawyer. He evaded all of it. Ace concocted all sorts of stories to tell at school, and everyone believed them. If anyone didn't believe his side, they kept it to themselves, which is often just as bad as believing it.

"So here we are. A year later. Going to our Christian school with him. Acting like nothing happened. My parents felt it was important to stay even though he got away unscathed. "

Felix sat watching me for a long moment, then wrapped me

up in his lanky arms and leaned his head on mine. "You don't have to act like it didn't happen. You are the bravest person I know. You are not that girl anymore. You've been through hell."

I felt relieved that Felix knew. "I haven't told anyone in a long while."

He kissed the top of my head. "I can tell that some of you is hardened because of this ordeal. I can tell where your sense of justice came from. I know why you don't trust people, and rightly so. But I just want to say that all of you has risen."

"I don't think you did that right," I whispered and giggled at the chance to turn that back on him.

He laughed. "You know what I mean."

"Yes. And thank you."

"Thank you for trusting me enough to tell me."

"You know I love you, right?"

"I know."

"I'm not saying you shouldn't write the article. What I'm saying is that there's a difference between covering the story and breaking the story," Mr. Knight said.

"Go on."

"Typically, reporters and papers are in a race to be the first to report. To be the one who breaks the story. But, in school journalism, you're not trying to beat anyone to the story. And, if you break the story, then, while you've done the right thing and exposed truth, I doubt anyone will trust you or confide in you anymore. And there's still two years left of high school for you."

"So, what, I just wait until it goes down?" I clarified.

"Not exactly. You have the story. You can *make* it go down, essentially. And be there to cover it at the right time when it does. With your partner, of course."

At just the mention of Nate, I grimaced, which Mr. Knight caught.

"What's up with you two, anyway?"

"Nothing."

He lifted one eyebrow and looked down at me.

"Okay. Not nothing," I admitted. "But I don't want to talk about it."

"Fair enough. Just continue to work together, okay?"

"Fine," I huffed.

Mr. Knight leaned back in his seat. "So, what do you think about what I've said?"

"I think it makes sense. But part of me still wants to break the story. It feels dishonest to pretend I didn't suspect or know this whole time."

"I admire that about you, Avery Brave. You always want to be truthful. Just think about it before you do anything, okay?"

"Okay."

A huge wave of relief washed over me as I left Mr. Knight's class. It felt good to have an adult know that I was very close to the truth about Mr. Hickham's list. Especially because several people felt threatened by that fact. I needed someone to vouch for me if, somehow, this all backfired.

That relief was short-lived. As I rounded the corner, I saw Sylvie, Ace, and Nate talking in a huddle in the middle of the hall. The sight of them made me fume, which Nate saw as he looked up just at the right time to see me glaring at him.

Felix grabbed my arm and pulled me toward the lockers. "Nothing to see there. Come on. I have something for you."

"Didn't you see him!? There's no denying it now."

"Let it go, or I think you'll explode."

I took a deep breath and tried to imagine punching Nate in the face, which made me feel guilty and, frankly, didn't help.

"Whatever you just tried didn't work. So maybe this will. I just saw one of the student governmentals in Mr. Hickham's office, and he was handing him a roll of cash."

"Don't joke. This isn't a drug deal."

"What if it is?"

I started to laugh and jab him, but then I realized he was serious. *Drug deals? Cash? Or...* What if they were paying him off for whatever inappropriate material he had on their phones?

"Felix, you're a genius!"

I turned to dart away down the hall. Felix grabbed my arm.

"Aren't you going to tell me what's going on now?"

"Can't. I'm on the cusp. This is huge. I need you to be my eyes and ear but have plausible deniability when it all goes down."

"Hey, you did that right!"

"Thanks. I gotta go. Want to come over tonight?"

"Can't. Family dinner to discuss treatment."

"Is that still a thing?"

"Yep."

I turned back to face him. "I'm sorry. I wish I could make them see what I see."

"Which is what?"

"You're funny, smart, loyal, and honest. You're good looking and outrageously tall. You're not a culture clone, you're sensitive, protective, and, above all, a superb friend."

"Thanks," he said, blushing. "I'll come over after dinner, if I can."

"Okay. Gotta run!" I said, jogging off toward my next destination.

I grabbed my notebook and scribbled questions as fast as I could. I was curled up on the last toilet in the bathroom. I needed for more intel, and this seemed to be the place to get it.

DID THEY ALL WITNESS SOMETHING TOGETHER? I wrote.

DID THEY ALL PARTICIPATE IN SOMETHING TOGETHER?

IS THE CONTENT ON ALL THE PHONES RELATED?

WHAT'S WORTH PAYING HICKHAM FOR?

I heard Sylvie come in with someone else whose voice I didn't recognize. They didn't go into a stall but stood at the counter.

"How much are you paying him now?" the new voice asked in a quiet tone.

"One hundred for the pictures and a hundred for Ace's video."

Okay, so Sylvie had questionable photos on her phone and a questionable video. *Ew.* And she was paying Hickham two hundred dollars a month? *Wowza. Talk about bank roll.* No need to be a drug dealer; just blackmail the Saints for their indiscretions. Perfect. And ironic. He was a stellar human being.

"How about you?"

"One seventy-five. It really gets me. Can't we just turn in Ace's video and blow this whole thing up in both their faces?"

"No," Sylvie insisted. "If I turn in the video, he'll tell the whole world about the baby. He'll ruin me."

"I thought he wanted you to come forward about the blackmail."

"He did until he realized that it would ruin him too. Just by association. The only way to bring down Hickham is to tell the truth. So, he changed his mind."

"You're in a tight spot."

"Yep. I wish the police could just find the videos but not release what is on them."

"That doesn't sound like something they can do. The public has a right to know, right? Plus, it's a Christian teacher at a Christian school. You know the vultures will eat that up."

"I know. It's just wrong that he keeps them in his briefcase everywhere he goes. What a sicko!"

"Ugh. I know. I don't want to talk about him anymore. Let's talk about Nate. He is looking really good lately."

"Yeah. He is."

They both cackled.

"Don't let Ace hear you say that."

"He probably wouldn't even care. He's still in love with Avery. Can you believe that? I wish I'd never cheated on Nate with Ace. Now, I'm with one who's still in love with her, and I still love one who's falling in love with her. I hate that girl."

Nate is not falling for me! I thought irately. *Are you kidding me? We can't even speak to each other right now!*

"Let's go. We're going to be late."

And they exited the bathroom.

I had to find out what the video was. Not that I wanted to watch it, but I needed to find someone who knew. Whatever the video was, those two girls were both being blackmailed for it, and Ace didn't want it out. I had been out of school for several months and couldn't think of anything that I had heard that fit this seriousness. Felix wouldn't know because he hadn't been at All Saints long enough. I had no desire to talk to Nate, and I knew Mr. Knight couldn't tell me if he knew. The only person who might know…was Carol!

I hurried home after school to see if I could Facetime with Carol and ask her what she knew. Her brown hair was pinned back away from her face and was at least three inches shorter than the last time I'd seen her.

She bobbed into view on the screen.

"You cut your hair!" I exclaimed excitedly.

"Yeah, you like?"

"Yes! It's cute!"

We caught up on school and friends and what life was like without each other before I asked about Mr. Hickham. I heard her mom call her from downstairs. Dinner would be ready in fifteen minutes.

"Okay, I had to see you because I wanted to ask if you remember anything happening at the end of the year, after I left, that involved Ace, a video, Mr. Hickham, and Sylvie? Possibly others?"

I asked my question, then waited pensively. Carol bit her lip while she thought. She looked around her room absently, and then, as if the idea had come in through her ear, she hit her temple and said, "Duh!"

I leaned forward and tapped my fingers on the desk.

"This may not be it," she continued, "but I remember rumors floating around about some big party that happened at the end of the year. I heard it was at Hickham's house…totally not appropriate. But soon after, the rumors got squashed and fizzled out. What if something happened at the party, and it got documented on phones? Maybe Hickham found out that there was proof, and he's is trying to cover it up by blackmailing all the students who may have proof on their phones."

"The theory fits. It's awful, but it fits. But Ace is the wild card. No pun intended. Wouldn't you think he would just pretend like he had no part in any of it?"

"Yeah, but there's video evidence…Neither he nor his dad can out-spin that."

"True," I said. Then I started thinking about how to get the evidence. I would need to get the phones. But then, I remembered what the girls had said in the bathroom: *"I wish the police could just find the videos but not release what is on them."*

"I think I might have a plan."

"Does is involve duct tape, a burner phone, and a passport to some remote island?"

"No…I'm not MacGyver. Mr. Knight doesn't want me to break the story, and my mom and dad want me to play it safe and let them be involved, so I have to think this through. But I think I have a plan that just might work."

"What does Nate think?"

I paused, thinking about what I'd said to Nate on the phone and the way I'd looked at him in the hall when I'd seen him huddled up with Sylvie and Ace. "We're not on speaking terms at the moment."

"What happened?"

I let out an angry breath. "He's the one who told Sylvie I'd seen the list. And just today, he was scheming with Ace and Sylvie. I'm pretty sure this whole thing was a charade."

"He's a football player. I don't think they do charades."

"Carol, be serious."

"Sorry." Her joking smile faded, and she looked at me solemnly. "I can tell you're hurt. I'm sorry. I know you were starting to like him. Which is a big deal."

"Yeah," I said flatly, pushing my bitterness further down into my stomach only to realize I was hungry. I didn't want to talk about Nate. Talking about him only made me think about him, and thinking about him only made me wish…. Never mind. It didn't matter now anyway. "I gotta go. I need to go help with dinner and talk to my parents about my plan."

"Okay." We both looked sad. "Bye."

"Bye."

I hurried downstairs to find my dad at the table reading a

book while Mother worked on dinner over the stove.

"How's Carol?" Mother asked cheerfully without turning around.

"She's good. She cut her hair."

"Oh?"

"Yeah. Can I help with dinner?"

"Thanks, sweetie, but I'm almost done. Why don't you sit with your father and tell us how things are going at school?"

I pulled my usual chair out and slid down into it. "That's actually why I came down. I think I have a plan about Mr. Hickham. I wanted to run it by you."

My father put his book down and slid his glasses down further on his nose so he could look at me over them. His thick, graying hair and his bifocal reading glasses made him look much older than he was.

I told them what Carol and I had talked about and explained what I'd heard in the bathroom from Sylvie. My father rubbed his chin thoughtfully, and Mother had stopped stirring the sauce and looked worriedly at me, holding the wooden spoon and dripping sauce on her apron. They hadn't quite believed my hypothesis the first time we'd talked about Mr. Hickham, but their faces told me that they believed me now. I told them my plan to go about exposing Mr. Hickham, the phones, and the blackmail—being there to witness and report on it but keeping the contents of the phones classified.

"Don't you think it will take more than a tip to launch an investigation?" my mother said, finally laying down the spoon and wiping off the dribbles of sauce that were now running down her apron.

"Well, yes and no. But you leave that to me. I'll work out the details if you all agree that this is the way to go."

My father was stoic for several minutes. The kitchen was silent except for the clock on the wall that marched on and the soft simmering sauce on the stove that would bubble up and burst on the surface. He shook his head slightly, and I slumped a little, thinking that I'd have to defend my plan or that we'd argue. But instead, the serious lines around his mouth faded and softened into a smile.

"You know, Avery Brave, no high school student should have to face this. But we named you Avery Brave for a reason, and I won't keep you from living up to it. You astound me with your perception and insight, though it borders on suspicion...." He paused and winked at me, knowing he was being gracious with the word "bordered"—we both knew that I was suspicious most of the time. "And your sense of justice is probably unrivaled among your peers. I commend you for your pursuit of truth even when it is somewhat dangerous, and, most of all, I commend you for including us. You have become such a champion after all that you have been through. We will help you, protect you, stand up for you, and applaud you in any way that we can."

I was stunned. I had anticipated fear and protest from his demeanor, but instead, he was just dumbfounded. And not only did he agree with my plan, he wanted to help.

Mother took off her apron and brought the pasta bowl to the table. "And with that, let's eat."

"Just be at my house at seven. Don't ask any more questions," I whispered to Felix as we stood alone by our lockers.

He lifted one eyebrow at me. "Fine."

"I have to go; I've been late or skipped too much lately," I said as I hurried off to class.

It turned out that I hadn't needed to hurry that fast, because we were only watching selected approved scenes of Saving Private Ryan in history class. I asked to be excused to go to the bathroom about halfway through the period. I took my time on the way to the bathroom until I heard Nate's voice calling out from behind me at the end of the hall. I jogged toward the bathroom; it was childish, but it felt satisfying to duck him. Until the door closed behind me, and I saw Sylvie. I boiled inside, glared at her, and slammed my stall door. Which was also childish but also semi-satisfying.

"Avery?" Sylvie said in a vulnerable voice that I'd never

heard before.

"My name is Avery Brave," I retorted.

She paused. "Really? I have to say the whole thing every time?"

"Yes," I answered flatly. *Why am I so upset with her? Just because they were talking in the hall? Am I worried they'll get back together? Focus, AB!*

"What do you want, Sylvie?"

"I'm ready."

My mind darted back to that day in the supply closet. Then, I had to try very hard not to think about the day when Nate and I were in the supply closet.

I had told her to let me know when she was ready.

"Oh?" I tested her, not sure that she wasn't somehow in cahoots with Nate and Ace. Then, I laughed to myself for thinking the word "cahoots" and knew that Felix would laugh at me.

"I'm done being under everyone's thumb. Can you come out and talk?"

I smirked at her from behind the stall door. "No. It's not safe to talk in here."

"It's a bathroom," she sneered.

I opened the door and gave her a snide look. "You never know who's listening in a bathroom." I winked at her, and she looked baffled. "Come to my house at seven." And I left.

Either Sylvie was on board or she was in for a sour surprise tonight. Only time would tell.

"What are you so pleased with yourself about?" Nate laughed. "It looks pretty funny, you coming out of the bathroom with that kind of smile on your face."

My smile dropped right off my lips. Nate was standing by the water fountain, waiting on me to come out. He no longer had a cast on, just a black boot velcroed on the outside of his jeans. He still had his crutches tucked under his arms.

"Leave me alone, Nate." I turned back toward my classroom, trying to walk briskly away and hoping he couldn't keep up. But I guess, now that he could put some pressure on his boot, he could go much faster. He caught up with me, surprisingly, and grabbed my elbow, which sent a shock down my forearm. I snatched my arm back and spun toward him. "What do you want?"

"Why are you avoiding me?"

"You know why! You told Sylvie."

"I thought we were friends. I can't believe you would think I would do that."

"I don't know what we were, but we're not anymore," I said coldly.

"Well, I didn't tell Sylvie."

"Do you think I'm an idiot?"

"No!" He raised his voice, which made me feel like I was fuming out of my ears.

"You are the only person who knew about that. I thought I could trust you!" I shouted back at him.

"Ms. Nightingale!" Ms. Midler scolded as she scurried toward us. "Stop shouting in the hallway."

"Look what you did," I hissed at Nate. "Now, we're going to get detention."

His face reddened, and his eyes filled with some expression that was a mixture of shame and fury.

"You two leave me no choice to but to give you afternoon detention. You're supposed to be in class, not out here in the hallway. And certainly not yelling at each other. These are not character traits of a Saint."

"You're right, Ms. Midler. Please forgive me," I said stiltedly.

"Actually," she said, "I need to see you in my office before detention, Avery Brave."

"Yes, ma'am."

She handed us each a detention slip, and we both took a walk of shame back to our classroom. I felt myself huff everywhere I went the rest of the day. I was annoyed that Sylvie was either toying with me or actually turning out to be a decent person. I felt angry that Nate would betray my trust and still try to get close to me, and, what was more, he'd gotten me into detention. And I was anxious about tonight.

As I turned in my article to Mr. Knight, I stood at his desk while the other students filed out. Nate was gathering his things rather slowly and keeping an eye on me, I could tell. With my back to him, I whispered, "It's 'all happening at seven tonight. I don't expect you to come. I just wanted you to know. We even have someone possibly willing to come forward and testify."

Mr. Knight nodded silently and went back to looking at my paper so he wouldn't look conspicuous. Nate followed me out and loudly crutched after me all the way to the room where detention was held. I passed the door and headed toward Ms. Midler's office. She was waiting for me by the door.

"Quickly, now. We both need to get to detention. I just needed to speak with you."

I sat down on the edge of the seat, not intending to settle in.

"I've heard pieces of conversations from several students about a certain incident involving you and Ace Wentworth last year. And also some rumors about this year. I just wanted to let you know that there are certain areas of the school that a under surveillance for your safety," she said cryptically.

"Cameras."

She nodded.

I tapped my fingers thoughtfully on my knee. "How would one go about getting footage?"

"School regulation is that footage can be released with a police-issued warrant," she said, folding up her cardigan sleeves, which revealed the edges of tattoos. "Now, off we go. We both have detention waiting."

I stood to follow her out, but I needed to let me parents know about my detention. I pulled out my phone as Ms. Midler and I walked toward the designated room. I stopped just outside the door to call Dad.

"Hey, Dad. I have detention. Just wanted to let you know I'd be late."

"Avery Brave—my word! Why on earth do you have detention?"

"Ms. Midler caught Nate and me yelling at each other in the hallway during class."

"Okay…well, you can explain that one to me later. How late will you be?"

"Just an hour. Everything is still a go for seven."

"Okay. See you then."

"Bye, Dad."

"Don't yell at anyone else."

"No promises," I said jokingly and then ending the call.

I chose a seat as far away from Nate as I could get. He noticed and shook his head. Yes, I was being childish again, but my Father *had* told me not to yell at anyone else. I figured the only way I wouldn't yell at Nate Reinhart would be to get as far away as possible.

"Ms. Midler," Nate spoke up, "I forgot my notes from newspaper in my locker. Can I go get them?"

Ms. Midler eyed him skeptically and then looked at me. "Ms. Nightingale, aren't you two writing partners this semester? Can you help Mr. Reinhart out with his notes?"

"I don't think that is wise. Considering he's the reason I'm here," I protested.

"Mr. Reinhart, why don't you go sit by Ms. Nightingale and share her notes?" Ms. Midler sighed, sounding exhausted.

Nate tried hard not smile as he gathered his stuff and hopped over to the desk next to mine. I glared at him as he slid down into it.

"Nice. Really smooth, Reinhart." I fired my words at him like whispering arrows.

"What's going on at seven?"

"Wha—?" *How could he know?* "What do mean?"

He leaned across the space between our desks as if he was looking at my notes. "I heard you on the phone just now, and I heard you and Sylvie in the bathroom."

"You were listening to our conversation in the bathroom?" I retorted, offended.

"What? You do it all the time! I was just taking a lesson from you."

I threw my head back and rolled my eyes. He had a point, which made me even more irritated.

"So…what's happening at seven?"

When I looked back at him, he was closer to my desk than I

anticipated, and our faces were a pencil's length away from each other. My breath caught. I could smell the soap from the locker room and the mint on his tongue. His eyes were fixed on mine, and, for the first time, I realized they looked like fading denim.

For a moment, I was mesmerized and forgot to be mean. I saw the light freckles just under his eyes, invisible until I was this close. His thick eyes brows weren't nearly as expressive as Felix's, but they were currently stretching and reaching for his forehead in surprise at me. Because I was staring. He was staring, and I was staring.

"I don't trust you enough to tell you," I whispered.

"What do I have to do to make you believe that I didn't tell Sylvie? I told you that I don't talk to Sylvie."

"You were talking to her in the hall—with Ace, no less," I said bitingly.

His eyes suddenly switched from staring at me pensively to defensive. "That was about something else entirely. And if you must know..." He paused.

"Yes! I must know."

He glared at me in annoyance. "The water boy was in on their original blackmail plan. He was trying to get the list as well. He saw you in the field house that night. He's the one that told Sylvie. Not me."

I blinked and shuffled my feet under the desk uncomfortably. It sounded plausible. But how could I know he was telling the truth? He could easily make that up. Sylvie could have told him about tonight. It could all just be a game. How could I trust him?

My Father was right; I was suspicious all the time. Did I have reason to be? Sure. But did I wish I could trust him and let him go on looking at me this way? *Sure.*

"Maybe that is the truth, maybe it's not. You want to know what you have to do to make me believe you? You'll have to get me proof."

We had been talking so low that we hadn't seen Ace walk into the room, but he lorded over Nate's desk now. My eyes flew to the teacher. She was grading papers and apparently had not seen him enter so stealthily.

"I thought I told you to stay away, Ace," Nate said flatly, though I thought it best he not speak at all. I found my body moving slowly out of my desk and away from them, towards the corner.

Ace's two hands grabbed Nate's shirt collar and yanked him out of his seat. "If anyone needs to stay away from her, Reinhart, it's you!"

Ace and Nate toppled to the floor, bringing books and desks with them. Nate struggled against Ace, and Ace struck blows at the sides of Nate's ribs.

"Get off me, man!" Nate shouted breathlessly as he rolled with Ace.

"Stay away from her!"

"She's not yours!"

I felt like the fight slowed and was suddenly moving slow motion. Nate shoved Ace off of him, and Ace hit his back on the desk where Ms. Midler sat, causing her to jump up, shriek, and grab her walkie-talkie to call for help. Ace lunged at Nate again. They were fighting over me? *Is Nate fighting Ace right now? If they were planning something together, they wouldn't fight over me. Would they?*

But my thoughts were cut short, and I covered my ears as Ms. Midler blew what sounded like a foghorn.

"Everyone out. Detention is dismissed. Except Mr. Wentworth and Mr. Reinhart. You two will be staying."

I scrambled to grab my books and my backpack and hurried from the room. *Weirdest detention ever.* I caught Nate's eye just before I filed out of the room with the other kids. His expression was one I'd never seen.

Of course, Mother had insisted on having snacks. So, there were brownies, chips and dip, and trail mix all spread out on the table as we sat around it. Felix sat there snacking and talking to Carol, who had her own digital place at the table, while Sylvie sat silently next to me, picking at her cheer uniform.

My Mother and Father waited in anticipation for me to call our secret meeting to order. We were originally supposed to only be five, but now, with Sylvie, we had six. And that was even better. It was ten after seven, and before we began, I wanted to test Sylvie once more.

"Sylvie, can you help me get some drinks from the cooler in the garage?"

"Uh, sure," she said awkwardly as everyone watched us rise from the table and leave.

As we walked out into the garage, I flicked the light switch on and stopped.

"Sylvie, why the change of heart?"

"What is this, some sort of intervention?"

I laughed. "No. I can see why you thought that, with the snacks and all…," I said sarcastically, "but no. It's something else entirely. But I need to be sure of you before you are privy to that information."

"Sure of me? Privy? Who are you, Sherlock Holmes?"

"Hardly. That man was a brilliant literary work of fiction."

"Whatever. I'm here because you told me to be here. And I came to you because you told me to, when I was done being—you know."

"And?"

"What else do you want me to say, Avery Brave?!" she demanded in a shaky voice.

"I want to know whose thumbs you were under and why."

Sylvie burst into tears and buried her face in her hands. "At first, it was just Ace. He could practically hang me with what he had on me." She sobbed and hiccupped. I put my hand on her shoulder as she continued, feeling slightly guilty for pushing her. "As if going through it wasn't traumatic enough…then, it was Hickham for what I had on my phone, and then Hickham again for what we'd recorded at the party."

There it was. She was guilty on all three counts for indiscretions that Saints Academy would surely crucify her for. Metaphorically, of course. But along with her crimes was the proof to take down not just Mr. Hickham but Ace Wentworth.

I hesitated before deciding to hug her. I chose a side hug, though it felt just as awkward as I thought a full hug would have.

"I'm sorry," I said sincerely. "None of this is okay. And I know we're not good friends, but I am sorry that this has been happening to you."

I knew it was a technicality to call someone an acquaintance versus a friend or even a good friend, but I decided to let it go for the sake of the cause.

Sylvie hiccupped again and looked at me. "Do you think God will forgive me for what I've done?"

My heart broke open for a girl I could barely tolerate most any other day. But today, standing in my garage, I knew we weren't that different. We were a few choices away from being quite similar, actually.

"I know for a fact that he will." She shook her head as if she couldn't believe it. So, I added, "He already has, and he always will. He kinda can't *not* forgive you." I patted her arm. "I know you know that, but I get it that it's hard to believe sometimes when all the shame shouts louder."

Sylvie lifted her head enough to wipe her nose on her uniform, which was gross, but I couldn't blame her…we were in a garage.

"I don't think you did that right," she said, which made me laugh a little and think of Felix, who was in my kitchen with my parents and Carol. I hoped they were okay. "But I think I know what you mean," she finished.

It was a do or die moment, and I took a deep breath. "Sylvie, the reason that we're here tonight…I mean, the reason I asked you to come tonight is because we're going to call the authorities, the media, and whoever we think needs to know. We're hoping this is the proper way to bring Mr. Hickham and Ace Wentworth to justice."

"And you want *me* to tell them?"

"Only if you are up for it. We're all doing it anonymously. Just reporting it and letting them investigate and break the story, you know. You can tell your side if you want, but I know you're worried about it ruining your future."

"You know, don't you?"

"I do."

"Let me guess, overheard in the bathroom?"

I shrugged. I thought about Nate rolling on the floor with Ace. If he was willing to fight for me, then the least I could do was not out him as my source. Even if I was still upset with him.

"Then I bet you heard all that stuff about me and Ace and you and Ace and you and Nate."

"There is no me and Ace," I jumped in, a little too eager.

"Well, I'm sorry I said all that. I was just jealous. I hate what I did to Nate. And I hate the power Ace has over me." She paused, looking hesitant to say more. "And, for the record, I'm sorry about what happened to you last year. I hate the way everyone treated you. You're doing the right thing tonight for people who didn't do the right thing for you last year."

I felt myself flush but kept my face impassive. "It's okay," I said, shrugging again. Hearing the words I'd wanted someone to say for a whole year come out of Sylvie's mouth was bittersweet. "Come on. It's time."

We walked back to kitchen and rejoined the table; the group was currently engaged in an intellectual debate—which was better, the original Lone Ranger or the remake.

"Guys—it's time," I interjected. They all quieted and pulled out their phones. "Should we pray first?" I asked, but before anyone could answer, the doorbell rang.

"Did you invite anyone else?" My father asked with slight concern.

"No...," I said, letting the word trail off as I walked toward the front door. I opened the door cautiously, silently praying it wasn't Ace or Mr. Hickham.

Nate stood before me, out of breath and with a swollen right jaw. He held a briefcase out to me.

"What's this?"

"Proof," he said in between his panting breaths.

"Did you run here? And proof of what?"

"You said..." He took in a huge breath and let it out slowly. "You said I had to get you proof for you to believe me. To know what side I'm on. Here's your proof."

"I don't get it."

"It's Hickham's briefcase."

"What?!" I said too loud. Everyone came running into the foyer; Felix even held Carol on the iPad.

"What's going on?" Nate looked at everyone, bewildered that they were all here, especially Sylvie. "I mean, I guess I did come around seven, but what's happening?"

"We're tipping off the police. Want to join us?" Felix answered before I had a chance.

"Hold on!" I raised my voice. "This wasn't in the plan. This is a major kink. We all need to talk in the kitchen." I pulled Nate inside by his shirt sleeve. *He brought me proof. He brought me the proof we needed. He brought me proof.*

I wanted to hug him. I wanted to pull him out into the garage like I had Sylvie and make him tell me everything. And hug him. But there wasn't time for that.

We gathered around the table again, and everyone was looking to me. I felt stunned and blank, so I took a brownie and shoved it in my mouth. Felix followed suit, I assume just so I didn't look like an idiot.

"What's the kink, dear?" Dad started. "Is it just that you didn't expect this boy to be here?"

"Sorry! This is Nate. Nate, these are my parents, and Carol's on the iPad. You know Felix and Sylvie..."

Nate nodded and smiled an embarrassed smile. *He even brought me proof, and Sylvie is here. Not that he knew she would be but still. He's bold. He has been loyal this whole time when I questioned him at every turn.* I thought back to the dance and to detention, when his face had been close enough to smell. My face was growing pink up the sides; I could feel it.

"No, Nate has brought me—us—the briefcase that supposedly contains the confiscated phones. How did you get this?" I said, turning to Nate, who towered behind me.

He shrugged as if it was no big deal. "Once they figured out that I had nothing to do with instigating the fight today, they let me go and walked Ace up to the principal's office. I went back to the locker room to get my bag, and Mr. Hickham's briefcase was just sitting on the desk. So, I grabbed it before I even thought about it."

My mother chimed in in a rather squeamish voice, "Isn't that stealing, dear?" She gave me a look. "I thought we were going to do this the proper way?"

"I know. That's the kink," I announced. "We were just going to call anonymously, not to have any proof. They had to do the finding. I even found out the school has footage. We could show Ace violating his restraining order, assaulting Nate, Hickham's dealings...we would have had proof of everything. But *they* were supposed to find. We weren't supposed to deliver it. So, no what?"

Nate leaned over behind me and whispered into my hair, "I'm sorry. I wasn't really thinking. I just wanted to get you proof."

"Sorry. Talk amongst yourselves. Excuse me," I said as I tugged on Nate's sleeve to follow me back into the foyer. I scolded him in a whisper. "Don't apologize. I'm not mad. Just confused. Okay?"

"Okay."

"I have a plan!" Sylvie yelled from the kitchen. We re-entered the room with surprise.

"We'll all call, as planned. But part of our tip is that we have a witness who will come forward with the proof they need as long as they can meet some conditions."

"But we don't," I stated the seemingly obvious.

"Yes, we do," she said. She let her words hang in the air. "I will take the briefcase to the station and give my full report."

I knew my eyes were wide, but they didn't match the size of Nate's.

"Sylvie? You would do that? What about—"

She didn't let me finish. "I know. I'll cross that bridge when I get to it. But in light of the rest of the trouble I'll be in, a little slap on the wrist for stealing the briefcase won't matter. I wouldn't want anyone else to get into trouble over this," she said, looking to Nate, which I felt oddly uncomfortable about. "Let's just pray that they investigate and report without divulging what is on the phones. Maybe I can testify if they promise to meet our conditions."

"Dear, that is very brave," my father said. "We will support you however we can in the aftermath."

There as a moment of silent pause as we all started to see Sylvie and her struggle in a new light.

"Okay, then," I said, sitting down. "It's time. Let's go over the facts once more. We have a key witness willing to testify that Mr. Hickham has been blackmailing students, forcing them to pay him to keep the contents of these phones secret, among other inappropriate actions by Mr. Hickham. Everyone on board with that?"

Everyone nodded. Nate sat down at the end of the table by Felix, and I tried not to read anything into it. We all took out our phones and dialed. Some of us called the newspaper, some of us called the news station, some of us called the police.

It was done.

I laid on my bed thinking about the inevitable aftermath of the afternoon's events. Our school would be rocked. Sylvie's parents would learn the truth and most likely be devastated. Ace would be in the news once again. And, with any sort of providence, the police would find video proof and finally send him to jail. And every person on the list would be free of the hold that Mr. Hickham had on them.

As I drifted off to sleep, I thought about Nate bringing me the proof I had told him I required in order to believe him. He stole Hickham's briefcase to show me that I could believe him. And, while stealing shouldn't really be a proof of honesty, today, it felt like it was. He'd brought me pie once and now a stolen briefcase. I didn't quite know what it all meant, but I suppose it meant that I believed him.

The next morning, I had seventeen text messages. Sylvie was freaking out and didn't want to wait until after school to go to the police, like we'd agreed on. She wanted to go first thing in the morning before she lost her nerve or before Ace could get to her. And she wanted me to drive her there. She would call her parents after it was all done to have them come get her and, of course, explain. She thought it better to do it after than before because they might try to stop her. All of this via text message before 6:30 in the morning!

I got my breakfast to go and explained everything to Mom and Dad on my way out the door. They told me they would pray and asked me to check in after the station. I picked Sylvie up outside the gate of her house. She looked a little nauseated.

"You ready?"

"Yeah, but ramped up. This is big. Right?"

"Yeah. It's pretty darn big," I confirmed. "But you know it's what is right, right?"

"Yeah, sure. I just feel like I'm giving up my whole future. But then again, I guess I sabotaged that a while back, didn't I?"

We were silent the rest of the way to the station, which was about a ten-minute drive from Sylvie's house. She suddenly turned to face me and told me to pull over.

"Are you going to vomit?"

"No, just pull over."

I eased the car into a parking lot and put it park. "What's the matter, Sylvie? Are you having second thoughts?"

"No!" she insisted a little too harshly. "I just need you to know what's on the phones before I do it."

"No—I don't—I think its best—," I stammered. "I don't need to know, Sylvie. It's none of my business. I'm doing this because what Ace and Mr. Hickham have done to you is wrong. Beyond that, I can't be anyone's judge. Heaven knows all the questionable things I've done."

"But that's the thing. The thing that Mr. Hickham will do anything to keep quiet is something that happened at his house. At the party."

"I know, I heard. But I don't really want or think I need to know details. I just want the police to find out. Not me."

"It's about Ace."

I laughed through my nose is a bitter way. "I'm not

surprised. What did he do this time?"

"It wasn't what he did. It's what Mr. Hickham did to him."

My mind felt like it tripped over her words and was sprawled out on my skull wondering what she meant. I couldn't even piece her words back together to make sense of them or what she was saying that she wasn't saying.

"Nothing like *that* happened," she clarified quickly, and I suppose the shock and horror on my face showed even though my mind couldn't think clearly enough to tell it what to express. "Some of us just caught Hickham coming on to Ace. Like big time. We all caught it on video. Hickham was drunk. Very drunk. They both were."

I pretended to push rewind. "Hold on. Let me make sure I have this straight. Hickham comes on to Ace at the party. You guys video. Hickham finds out that it's videoed and starts to confiscate the phones, blackmailing you guys to pay him so that he doesn't release the other questionable material he knew was on your phones? Which is honestly just a sad ironic byproduct of his plan. He probably came up with that after he starting to gather the phones, realizing he had several ways to shut you up."

I put my hands on my forehead as if trying to keep all the information in.

"I guess my only hang-up is Ace. Why didn't he just come forward and tell someone? Hickham would have gotten fired so fast last year, no one would have even seen it coming."

Sylvie folded and refolded the hem of her skirt. "Hickham vouched for Ace when he was accused of—well, you know. So, Ace always figured, if he ratted on Hickham, last year would come back to haunt him. And then the baby thing. He just found a way to control everyone. He always wants to have the upper hand."

I was the one who felt like vomiting now. Hickham had helped? *What kind of monster—? Never mind, I don't even need to think about that.* He was the type of person who would help a student get out of taking responsibility for his actions, and he was the type of person who would try to take advantage of a student.

As much as I wanted justice for Hickham and Ace, I felt an odd sense of regret. Was what we were about to do going to ruin lives, make more enemies, and sabotage the rest of high school? I looked at Sylvie, who clutched Mr. Hickham's briefcase as if it contained lost pirate treasure.

I knew it didn't matter. The truth had to prevail so that freedom could as well. No one should live in fear; I knew that firsthand.

I dropped Sylvie at the front door with one request: that she leave us out of it. She nodded and disappeared inside the front door where she was swarmed by officers; they were expecting her.

I drove away with a sense of relief that it was done. But it wasn't. Now, I had to go to school and face Ace and Hickham without tipping them off. I needed to mend things with Nate, and I needed to pay attention in Algebra, because my grade was slipping.

Later that day, Felix and I sat on a bench outside, picking at our lunches but not feeling particularly hungry. I knew something was wrong with him, and it wasn't just the heaviness of last night.

"You want to talk about it?" I offered, hoping that he would.

"My parents found a place they want to send me."

"A place? Like they are sending you to rehab or what?"

"Something like that. It's a Christian therapeutic center. They think it will help."

I shoved my lunch back in its sack forcefully but then took a breath. I wasn't mad, I realized as a tear sprang from my right eye, hot and determined as it traveled down my cheek. "You're leaving me?"

"It's just for a little while. I figured, if I do whatever they want and show them that they are important…but I'm just me, then they might leave it alone once I get back."

I didn't know what to think or say. I was angry at his parents, but I wasn't really; I felt sad and hurt for him and for me. Which was selfish, but I'd only just gotten him, and now they were taking him away.

"But hey," he added, "you never know—it might work, and I'll come back and be in love with you." He elbowed me like it was a joke, but it didn't feel like one. I just leaned my head over on his arm, and we sat in silence until lunch was over. As we walked back to our dark corner, I asked, "When do you leave?"

"This weekend. They found a place and got me in so quickly that they didn't want to wait until school was out. I'll have a tutor while I'm there."

I wanted to respond, but I was afraid that, if I did, more tears would come. I hugged him and told him it wouldn't be the last time.

As I was headed toward Mr. Knight's classroom, I got a text from Sylvie. The police were on their way to the school. I ran all the way to Mr. Knight's class and motioned for him and Nate to come out into the hallway.

"It's about to go down," I said. "I'm going to get in place."

"Okay. I don't want you alone. Nate, you go with her. I'll be in the front office. Be careful."

We both nodded and headed out to the front of the school. We hid around the corner where we would be able to see the police and television crew arrive, but they wouldn't see us.

"What's going to happen to Sylvie?" Nate whispered.

"I don't know. I'll call you after this is done."

"Ace has done enough damage," he gruffed. "It's time he got what he deserves."

"He will. It will all come out in the wash."

"How are you so sure? I mean, he apparently didn't get what he deserved last year."

"But this year, we have proof—"

I stopped before I said anything more, and my heart sped up as I realized how close Nate was standing to me, peering around the corner. My mouth opened to tell him everything, but my stomach churned. I wasn't ready. And thankfully, I didn't even have to.

Nate shushed me and pointed to the front of the school. Six police officers escorted a handcuffed Hickham to the curb where they waited for the squad car to pull up. I got out the camera and snapped pictures of them ducking his head and putting him in the back of the car. Nate grabbed my hand to hold me back until the streams of students came running out onto the sidewalk in a frenzy. We joined them and continued to take pictures of

Hickham in the back seat.

We asked for statements from several officers, and we even watched the TV crew film a spot as the squad car drove away. All the other students were hysterical and asking questions, and several girls were crying, but a small pocket of students was quietly conferring with relief in their eyes and a weight lifted from their shoulders.

Soon, Principal Sands came out and made a very diplomatic statement that didn't reveal anything and made everyone go back to class even though there were only twenty minutes left in the day. Mr. Knight gave us discreet thumbs up and told us to stay out front in case anything else was going to happen. We both knew he meant, Ace but we weren't sure we wanted to witness that.

We sat down on the curb and watched the students filter reluctantly back through the doors. But soon, my gaze was not on the students; it was on Nate. Something was still gnawing at me.

"Can I ask you something?"

"Sure," he said, not looking at me, continuing to watch the front doors.

"What were you talking to Ace and Sylvie about in the hallway?"

Nate dropped his eyes from the doors for a split second, his eyes stern and serious. Then, they returned to the doors. "You," he admitted.

"Me?"

"I told them to leave you alone."

A jolt went down my spine. "Or else?" I joked.

"Something like that. That's why Ace jumped me in detention. He didn't like being told to stay away."

I nodded even though I felt puzzled. Why would he threaten Ace and Sylvie if we weren't even speaking at the time?

As if he read my mind, he answered, "Things were just getting intense…." He dropped his head down to look at me. "I just didn't want anything to happen to you."

Nate's face was close to mine, because we'd been talking in hush tones. I hadn't noticed his proximity or his height until this moment when I found myself fixated on his lips. His perfectly full lips were slightly parted as if he was still hanging on the last word he'd said: "*you.*"

I tilted my head upwards into the shade of his Razorback hat and, without thinking, kissed his bottom lip. It seemed an automatic response to the fact that he cared. But it was a stupid response. I froze. There, with my mouth on his mouth, I froze. *What in the world, Avery Brave! What are you doing? He's not kissing you back; you've ruined everything! How are you going to get out of this one?*

I considered pulling away and covering my face with my hands in shame. I thought maybe I could cry...but it wouldn't be real. I toyed with the idea of slapping him, which was off course and just as ridiculous as kissing him. Then, all of the sudden, as I started to pull away, his hand was at the back of my neck, pulling me back in, and his mouth was on mine. He kissed, and I kissed back; I kissed, and he kissed back. The world melted into a swirl of watercolor, and, although I was aware that we were still sitting on the curb, I didn't care.

Nate Reinhart was kissing me.

10.

I waited for Nate like he asked at the entrance of the team locker room, feeling completely awkward as players walked out and gave me "the nod". Did they know? Had Nate walked in to get his gym bag and announced it right away? The locker room was a gross cesspool of testosterone that I didn't pretend to understand or identify with. Or were they just being hormonal boys and checking me out? Maybe Nate had more class than to announce he'd just kissed the nosy reporter.

After there was a lull in the stream of players exiting the locker room, I inched my way toward the doorway, wondering what was taking so long. I heard a scuffle of feet and gruff voices. I strained to listen past the loud vent when I heard a long crash...like locker doors. I hesitated to race in and find out what it was, because anybody knows locker rooms equal boys in towels—or nothing at all. Something I had no intention of seeing. But in my hesitation, I realized one person I hadn't seen come out: Ace!

I rushed through the entrance and saw Nate's crutches on the floor. Nate was pinned against the locker with Ace's hand at his throat, the other drawn up in a fist, primed for a right cross. Ace's face was painted for the pep rally in red and blue but twisted in jealousy, anger, and shock.

Not again.

Nate's eyes widened, and he tried to shake his head, but I stormed to the side of Ace and pushed his ribs.

"Ace! Stop this! Get off of him!" I shouted.

Ace's fist turned to a backhand and caught me right on my left cheek. I fell backward over the bench with my feet in the air. I held my throbbing cheek but scrambled back to my feet.

"You had no right!" Ace yelled.

I knew what he was yelling about, but I didn't respond. Nate thrashed and yelled, managing to get a hand free and connect a few licks with Ace's chest and arm. I jumped onto the bench and then onto Ace's back, pulling his hair and causing him to yelp and turn on me. I didn't let go; I clung to his back as he tried to claw me off and thrashed around until he slammed us up against the lockers, causing me to crumple to the floor and gasp for breath. But my diversion had allowed Nate to regain the upper hand, and, with one swift connection of his crutch to Ace's head, Ace fell limp to the floor.

Nate hopped over to me and crashed to the floor beside me. "Avery! Are you okay?"

I pulled away in pain as he touched my cheek, "I'm fine."

"No, you're not. It's already bruising. And you can't catch your breath. Do you feel like a rib is poking you?"

I tried to take a breath—*ouch!* "Yeah."

"I think he broke a rib. Stay here. I'm going to go get help."

I anxiously looked at Ace lying unconscious on the floor. Nate pushed the hair from my face. "You're right. It will take me too long to crutch over there. I won't leave you here with him. I'll call coach, and he'll call the police."

As he hobbled to his locker to retrieve his phone, I held my side and tried to breath. My nose tingled as if tears were forming, but they didn't. I closed my eyes and tried to focus on breathing.

Nate returned and slid down beside me against the locker. "They're on their way."

"Okay," I said flatly, realizing the adrenaline was wearing off.

"You're crazy, you know. I don't know any other girl who would rush Ace Wentworth in a boy's locker room."

I shrugged. It wasn't the first rash thing I'd done that day.

"It was pretty bad-A."

I smirked and rolled my eyes, "That's my middle name. Bad-A."

"No, but it is Brave. And you certainly are brave," he said seriously.

My nose tingled again, this time followed by burning eyes. I ducked my head so Nate wouldn't see, but he did anyway, and he carefully wiped the tear off my throbbing cheek. "I'm sorry...."

He didn't say anything. He took my hand and held it on his lap. I stared at our hands, fingers intertwined.

"He waited until all the guys had left and tackled me," Nate explained matter-of-factly. "Knocked the crutches out from under me. Yelling threats about keeping my hands off you. How we had no right to out him, Sylvie, and Hickman like that. How we ruined him."

Flashbacks to Ace's cruel hands flooded my memory, and I cringed. "I'm so sorry, Nate."

Nate lifted my chin so that I was forced to look at him. "Avery, don't be sorry. None of this is your fault. This is on Ace. And he'll get what's coming to him, just like you said. He actually just walked himself right into it this time."

"What makes you so sure now?"

He shrugged. I was quiet for a long time, hesitating over whether I should share something with him that I couldn't take back. Something I felt might change everything. It was a do or die moment.

"Last year...he threw me down the stairs," I muttered.

"What?" Nate's eyes searched my face, confused. Then, it seemed to register, and Nate growled, scrambling toward Ace where he was still lying unconscious. I grabbed his boot just before he was out of reach.

"Don't, Nate! The rest of this was self-defense. But that wouldn't be."

He hung his head and paused just inches away from Ace as the head coach walked in followed by the paramedics and police.

Within seconds, we were separated by medics, the principal, fireman, and policemen, giving statements, getting checked out, and calling our parents. I knew, once my parents were called, I'd be whisked away, and this strange moment I'd had with Nate Reinhart might be over. Forever. When we saw each other on Monday, it might all just go back to the way it was. Football star forced to do projects with the nosy reporter. Maybe that kiss had just been the adrenaline. Maybe he was feeling protective in the moment, but that could change.

Just before they rolled me out on a stretcher for X-rays of my ribs, I looked back at Nate, and he gave me a sad smile and waved. His eyes looked pained, and I wanted to reach out for him, but I didn't.

"Are you okay?" Felix said as I answered the phone before I could even saw hello. I rolled over on my side and winced, immediately rethinking the move. I managed to push myself up to sit against my pillow on my bed.

"I'll be fine."

"I'm sorry I couldn't be there for all the fallout."

I smiled. It was good to hear his voice. "Where are you? It sounds echo-y."

"I'm at the retreat center."

"What?!" I sat up straight, yelping over my rib. "You're already gone?"

"Yes, I got whisked away on Friday. We left right after school."

"I didn't even get to say goodbye," I said, tearing up with a definite shake in my voice.

"I know, doll. I miss you already. You know I would have it go this way."

"Well," I sniffed, "how is it?"

"It's not terrible. Everyone seems to be really nice. It's like being on a really condescending vacation with strangers."

"Sounds pretty terrible to me." I wiped my face.

"I'll be able to call you in the evenings."

"Please do."

"Miss you, AB. You're the best."

"Just come back to me, Felix," I said in a completely melodramatic Southern Belle voice.

"I shall return, my love, whence forth I came."

We both about died laughing, which hurt, and I fell over on the bed from the pain.

"I didn't do that right," Felix said as he tried to stop laughing.

"It hurts to laugh. You gotta stop."

"It's lights out anyway. I gotta go. I love you, Avery Brave. I'll talk to you tomorrow."

"Love you too. Bye, Felix."

I want to flop back dramatically, but I had ease myself gently against the pillows with a sigh, and it didn't have the same effect. *Felix is gone. Just like that, he's gone.* He'd be back, I knew, but I already felt lonelier without him.

11.

*WITH GREAT STRATEGY, THE QUEEN CAN MOVE
ABOUT THE BOARD AS SHE PLEASES.*

I skipped the game that night for obvious reasons. I stayed in bed most of Saturday, and Mom even let me stay home while they went to church on Sunday, which was a small newsworthy miracle in and of itself. I missed Felix already, but I knew I'd talk to him that night.

I called Sylvie. "How are you?" I asked, concerned.

"I'm glad it's over." She sounded drained but peaceful.

"How did your parents take it?"

"They were furious at me, devastated about the baby, and grateful to you."

"I'm sorry, Sylvie. What's going to happen?"

"They are moving me up to my aunt's in Maine. She's single but well connected, and they think that, if I get a change of pace and remove myself from all of this, then maybe I can still get into the school I want."

"Wow. How do you feel about that?"

"It's not what I want, but they made some good points, and I think I'll maybe, if I get out of here, I might be able to forgive myself."

We talked for a while longer, and I expressed my gratefulness for her courage.

"I am sorry we were never friends, Avery Brave. And I'm sorry I was never nice to you, and I'm sorry for everything you went through with Ace. I wish you all the happiness. You deserve it."

"You too, Sylvie."

After we hung up, I managed to come downstairs, though I winced in pain with every step. Mom had a roast in the oven that I could smell, and I figured she'd pass out if I set the table while she was gone, which would be fun to watch, so I did. Until there was a knock at the door.

Still a little shaken, I paused with a knife in my hand and contemplated taking it with me to open the door, but I set it down and went into the foyer to open the door. I could see Nate's height and his dark hair through the designer glass.

I took a deep breath. What was he doing here? I open the door halfway to keep out all of the morning stickiness.

"Hey," he said before I could even get anything out.

"Hey," I answered.

We stood there staring at each other for what must have been a whole minute. I replayed Friday's events, something I'd been doing since they'd happened. I wondered if he was doing the same. *Do boys even do that?* I wondered.

"What are you doing here, Nate?"

"I just wanted to come check on you."

"You could have just texted, you know."

"I know."

I felt the realization rise in my cheeks, which hurt on the bruised side. *He wanted to see me.* "I'm okay. I've got a rainbow face, and my ribs are all wrapped up, so I don't move too much. But other than that, I'm okay."

"So, going wake boarding this afternoon would be out of the question?" he said, smirking at me.

"Um, maybe I could just take that rib out and go," I teased back. I had been kind of wrong. Things hadn't completely changed. We weren't at school—we were at my house—but still, not everything had changed.

He took a step closer and reached for my cheek, barely brushing it with his fingers. "Does it hurt as bad as it looks?"

"Oh, thanks...," I said, joking, but he furrowed his brow at me.

"Don't," he said almost crossly. My cheeks flushed again. I had no idea how to be with this Nate. He wasn't angsty or angry.

"Sorry," I said, surprising myself. "It is pretty tender." I remembered how I'd looked in the mirror this morning, seeing the purple under my eye swirl with a green and yellowish shade all the way to my jaw line. "I always have bruised easy, though."

"Have you heard anything about anyone?"

"I just talked to Sylvie. She's okay. But I haven't heard anything besides that."

Nate was still standing close, looking down at me, but then he ducked his head slightly as he said, "It's funny how a kiss started this whole mess, but it's the only thing I can think about."

"A kiss didn't start this. Ace has always been..." I trailed off as he reached for my hand.

"What I was trying to say was...it's interesting that one of the things that finally brought Ace in was you. You're like his kryptonite or something—and, I can't quit thinking about kissing you. And I think I'd like to do it again."

I wished there was an "off" button for the flush in my cheeks; it was definitely on repeat. He was so close, towering over me; all I had to do was look up, and I was sure he would kiss me again. But the moment was lost as my parents pulled up in the driveway.

As I closed the door behind me so they wouldn't think we'd been in the house alone, he whispered, "Maybe later, then."

It sent a shiver up my spine that I had never experienced before. He let go of my hand and began crutching toward the garage. He was going over to talk to them? I followed in disbelief.

My father was first out of the car with a pleased but surprised look on his face, which made me wonder if he'd taken his blood pressure medicine this morning.

"Avery, is this the boy that saved you?" he said, heading straight for Nate though looking at me. I assumed he had forgotten him being here the other night.

Nate extended his hand to my father. "We took him down together, sir."

They shook hands, and my father patted him on the back as my mother joined them with her purse on her shoulder and her thick Bible cradled in her arms.

"Won't you join us for lunch, Nate?" Mom's accent drew out his name like a cat purring. I hadn't even had a chance to tell them about the kiss yet, but judging by their hospitality, they may not overreact after all. I wasn't sure any of us was ready for me dating again, but as I watched my parents and Nate walk up the front steps, I realized I may have been wrong.

"Thank you, Mrs. Nightingale. I'd love to."

Before we went inside, Dad grabbed my elbow, so I hung back with him a little. He wrapped his arm around me, and I put mine around his waist.

"It's not right to celebrate his consequences, but I did hear that they've actually charged Ace. They are serious charges, and he'll most likely get tried as an adult. He's getting justice. You are getting justice. Sylvie is getting justice. I don't want to celebrate it, but I am relieved, and I knew you would be too."

I sighed, hugging him as tears of relief fell down my freckled cheeks. *Thank you, God.*

"Why don't you kids take your pie on the porch?" Mother suggested. Dad smiled at me and waved us off. We took our plates and went out on the "front porch," as mother called it, though it was more of veranda or a small country in and of itself. I led us to the swing that my mother insisted on even though it required at least forty feet of rope just to hang the thing. But it did make for a nice place to sit next to Nate.

"So...," I started, wanting to ask the obvious question, "what made you want to meet the parents and stay for lunch?"

He took a bite the size of Texas and then smiled. "One of the guys bet me that I couldn't get invited to lunch at the Nightingales'."

I elbowed him in the side. "I'm sure that is not on the top of the dare list," I joked back. He almost choked on his next bite of cherry pie. I slapped him on the back jokingly until he could take a deep breath. He laughed deeply, and it was a sound I wished I could record.

He still hadn't answered my question. I took a bite of my pie and then set it aside. Mother loved cherry pie; I preferred apple.

"I got to thinking that I wanted your parents to know that I wasn't just some guy. And even though I have been here a time or two before, it was always related to articles or whatever you want to call what we all did. A case?"

"Are you not just a guy?"

He set his pie aside and put his arm on the back of the chair. "I know I have been. But what if I thought I didn't want to be?"

"Not be just some guy?" I repeated him even though I'd heard him the first time. Loud and clear. "I…would need to think about it."

"I can handle that," he said, taking his arm off the seat behind me and leaning forward on his knees. I wasn't the nuzzling sort, but I realized when his arm was practically around me that there was a niche that was the perfect size for me right under his shoulder. I hadn't been in it, but I realized it was there, and now, it was gone. He looked contemplative for a moment and then looked at me from the side. "Is it because of me or Ace?"

I looked away, feeling the tingle in my nose and silently cursing myself for suddenly sprouting tear ducts in the last month. I looked out toward the yard, still wet with dew even though it was noon. I said, "Ace," but I couldn't bring myself to look back at him.

It was quiet for a while, and we could hear the cicadas out already today, creating a pulsing rhythm from the trees.

"I haven't really dated anyone besides Ace," I forced myself to explain. "He—"

"You don't have to tell me yet if you don't want to."

I caught my breath on his "yet" and suddenly felt brave enough to tell him, knowing his "yet" meant he wasn't going anywhere. "You know most of it, I suppose, indirectly. He fooled us all. My parents. Me. Everyone. He appeared ideal." I paused, choking down the lump in my throat.

So many times last year, I had tried to tell the truth, but no one would listen. I had told Felix, and the truth came easier now, but I felt nervous to let Nate in.

"He pressured me to have sex," I said, clearing my throat after I said it as if the words themselves irritated my throat. "He pressured me often and not very nicely. It started small. A grab that was too tight. A slap that was immediately apologized for. I got good at covering for him. No one would have believed me anyway. A good Christian boy would never hit a girl. But the night I caught him with Sylvie, he started going berserk and beating me. I tried to get away, but he threw me down the stairs." I let out a long breath. "That's the gist," I said softly.

Nate sighed and hung his head, shaking it. Was he disappointed in me? Would he change his mind?

"I remember his family made him untouchable," he said.

"Yep. We pressed charges, but they didn't stick. And turns out Hickham played a part as well."

"Son of a—"

"Don't." I put my hand on his forearm. "He's not even worth it. Even at the beginning of this year, I would have said that I wanted God to open the earth and have the kraken eat him or something gross, but this whole ordeal has made me realize that he may not pay for what he did to me, but what he did to Sylvie was worse. And I'd rather her get the closure that she needs than me."

Nate opened his mouth the say something, but his phone rang in his pocket. He mouthed *"sorry,"* and I got up and walked over to the front steps to let him talk. When he returned, he apologized again. "I'm sorry. This is literally the worst timing. My mom needs me for something. I'm sorry I have to leave. I don't want to leave. Can I come back later?"

"Umm," I said, feeling shocked at his response, "sure, it's fine."

I wasn't masking my disappointment well. *What happened to his 'yet'?* The certainty that he wasn't going anywhere came crashing down. Had I done something wrong? Was he judging me for what happened with Acc? Had he changed his mind about me? Was he just uncomfortable hearing about it?

I thought all of this but said none of it. Nate excused himself to say goodbye to my parents, who I'm sure were sitting at the table pretending not to be keeping an eye on us. When he reappeared, he promised to call before he returned, which I thought was thoughtful and polite, unlike what he'd done earlier, which was just show up at my door. Which I secretly liked. But I probably shouldn't tell him that.

"Are you sure that's a good idea, dear?" Mother asked, worried about my still-healing ribs.

After Nate had left, we'd just sat on the couch together, and I had explained everything that had happened—from the assistant principal to Felix to Nate. And now, I just wanted to slip beneath the water for a minute and relax in the soundless cool fluidity. "I just want to get in; I'm not going to swim laps."

My father chuckled and kissed me on the head. "We're going to bed. Enjoy the pool. Thanks for telling us about Nate. We like him. Just take it slow. We love you."

"Thanks, Dad. G'night, Mom," I said as hugged her around her thin waist, and she kissed my cheek.

We hadn't always been so close. There was a time I was too afraid to tell them anything, especially the truth, but that had all changed when Ace and I broke up. Now, I was grateful that I could tell me parents anything, even about a boy kissing me or my best friend being sent away.

I continued to think about how much things had changed between my parents as I slipped into my suit and grabbed my towel. Turning off lights as I went through the house, I turned on the pool lights and the party lights that Dad had installed last summer. The pool was warm but still somehow refreshing in the heat. I waded out till the water covered my stomach, and then I carefully sunk down beneath the water, feeling enveloped, overtaken by the cool depths.

I held my breath and relaxed, slowly floating back to the surface. I desperately wanted to swim, but I know I couldn't stretch my side out enough when even reaching up to brush my hair had felt impossible. I floated in the surface with relaxed limbs and stared up at the stars that were still visible past the party lanterns' glow.

With my ear just below the water, the cicadas were slightly muted—and so was my phone that was ringing on the lounge chair. The sounds blended together beneath the water, and I didn't distinguish between the two. But then, I heard a truck door shut. Trying to stand upright again felt like thrashing, but I finally got out of the pool and grabbed my towel.

Reminding myself that Ace was currently in police custody and I had nothing to be nervous about, I cautiously peeked my head through the gate, my wet hair dripping on the walkway. It was Nate's truck. His eyes widened as he saw me at the gate sopping wet, wrapped in a towel. But his shock dissolved into a smile that sent an electric pulse through my heart that I knew was dangerously close to pleasure.

"I thought you were going to call," I half-whispered.

"I did," he said, coming so near that I could smell his cologne. He'd showered recently, which caused me to wonder what he'd had to go do all afternoon.

"Oh," I said softly, "I guess I didn't hear it when I was in the pool."

He looked at the towel. I felt my face blush. *Maybe I should go change*, I thought even as my legs felt as if they were turning to cement.

"How's your rib?"

"Oh. It's okay."

"Is it bruised too?" he asked.

I pulled my towel barely to the side, open just enough to show him the nasty purple swirl that almost looked like a bad tattoo on my side, seeming to connect my swimsuit bottoms with the top.

He clenched his teeth; I could see his jaw muscles grind as he stared at my side. I closed my towel, and he looked up to my uncomfortable expression. He was both worried and protective. I could see it in his brow.

"Maybe I should go change."

He didn't want me to—I could feel it—but he said, "Okay."

I pulled my hair around over one shoulder and wrung the water out. "Stay right here," I said as I turned to go inside.

But Nate grabbed my arm before I could walk away. "Wait."

As I turned around, he was close. Too close. I was suddenly very aware that I was in a bathing suit and a towel.

"Nate, I really should change." I remembered the pleasure in his smile and the electricity between us.

He was towering over me like he had been on the front porch earlier today. His breathing was shallow, and his blue eyes intensifying. "I might lose my nerve."

Hearing the whispering echo of the "maybe later" that he had said on the porch earlier today, in my head, I knew what he meant, but I knew I didn't want to feel ashamed about it later.

"If that's the case…" I paused momentarily. Maybe this wasn't fair after my impulsive kiss on Friday, but I reminded myself that no one was half naked then. "Maybe it's best," I finished as I pulled away from him and ducked in the back door.

I returned within minutes in a t-shirt and jean shorts with my hair wadded on the top of my head. Nate wasn't by the pool where I'd left him. *Great, he left.* The gate was open, and I wandered through it, sure that his truck would be gone.

But there, against his matte black hood and grill, he leaned with his arms crossed, his crutches leaning next to him. Waiting for me. Even if it meant he'd lost his nerve, he'd stayed. I liked that.

I joined him, leaning against the hood. "Thanks for waiting."

He just nodded.

We stood there, side by side, for a while in silence until he said, "Sorry I had to leave earlier."

"It's okay."

"I felt like we were in the middle of something. Once I got home, I realized my mom didn't need me that desperately, and I should have just stayed, and all I could think about all day was coming back."

"It's really okay. Did you have a good afternoon?"

"Not especially. Mom fired the landscaping guy again but had some event planned for tomorrow, and she needed Tan and me to get the yard ready."

"I heard Tanner played well in the game on Friday."

"Yeah, I heard that too."

So he didn't go.

"Do I need to go? Will your parents be upset that we're out here?"

You didn't seem to care about that when I was in a swimsuit, I thought but said, "No, they are already asleep. My dad doesn't like me to be alone in the house with...boys." I paused, thinking this was an awkward turn in the conversation. "But we're fine out here."

He nodded. "Neighbors can see and whatnot?"

"And whatnot," I repeated. Then, I found myself whispering, "Did you lose your nerve?"

Nate shook his head and laughed. "No."

"Okay, good. I just didn't know if my jeans shorts were so off-putting that you'd decided against...," I joked, trailing off at the end.

"Not necessarily. I got to thinking while you were gone that you were right. If I lost my nerve just because the moment passed, then maybe I shouldn't be doing it. And I didn't want you to think that I only wanted to kiss you."

"Not only?" I raised one eyebrow teasingly, though I knew he hadn't meant it that way.

"Why do you do this to me? It's been this way since the beginning; I say things I don't really mean, and I mean things I can't really say."

I smiled and found myself wanting to reach for him. It was probably best that the crutches were between us.

"What I meant was I want to kiss you again. I might even tonight. But I wanted to ask you to go on a date with me. A real one. I know we've been spending a lot of time together recently, but I want to spend time with you on purpose now. If that's okay. I know you said you needed to think about it."

I looked over at him and smiled, nodding a yes. I realized I'd been wrong. The whole time, I'd been wrong.

"Did you hear about Ace?" I asked, changing the subject to cover my blush.

"I did. Do you feel relieved?"

"Yes. I'm ready to move on from this whole ordeal."

"I'm glad," he said sincerely. "So, it's a yes on the date?"

"Yes," I confirmed out loud.

Nate grinned at my response. "I have to be out of the house tomorrow for my mom's JA event. I'll come pick you up."

"Okay," I said, then heard my phone ringing inside the gate by the pool. "Hang on, let me grab that." I jogged in my bare feet inside the gate and snatched up my phone. I swiped "answer" as I said, "Hey, Felix."

Felix immediately launched into some story about a documentary he'd just finished. I laughed until I saw that Nate had followed me inside the gate and limped toward me. His blue eyes flashed in the light of the lanterns, and his brown hair curled at the edges as it grew damp from the sweat on his neck. *He is surely the most attractive boy I know*, I thought.

While I still held the phone to my ear and made the occasional "uh-huh" to Felix, Nate stared into my eyes and put his hand behind my neck. A smile spread across his lips, and I knew he was going to kiss me.

"Felix...I'm gonna have to call you back...," I said into the phone and then dropped in on the lounge chair as Nate bent to kiss me, pulling me close with his hand that was on my neck and then in my hair. As I let him kiss me, I felt my heart race. I couldn't really breathe, but I didn't care, because Nate Reinhart was kissing me again, and this time, it felt altogether something like jazz and fireworks.

"So, Ace is really gone?" Felix asked, his wide eyes accentuated by the Facetime angle.

"Yep. Gone."

"How does that feel?"

"Freeing."

"And how was the date?"

"It was good," I said vaguely.

"That can't be all," he demanded.

"You're fishing."

"You're avoiding."

"You're barraging."

"You're stalling."

"You're..."

"I'm amazing and funny, and you miss me."

"I do."

We smiled at each other, feeling our friendship over the distance and thankfulness flooding me. Then, Felix continued. "So, what's next for the All Saints Queen?"

I laughed at the thought of me as Homecoming Queen. "Finishing sophomore year," I said simply. "Trying to survive without you. What about you?"

"Coming home in a month. Hoping to all that is holy that you haven't moved on without me."

"Never could."

"Me neither."

I had no idea what would become of me and Nate. I had no idea if Felix's parents would accept him when he returned. No one knew what would happen to Mr. Hickman and Ace in prison. I wondered if Sylvie would find forgiveness and happiness. I wasn't sure I could pull up my math grade or what the rest of my sophomore year would hold.

I didn't know much, but I knew I had been dreading this year, feeling like I didn't have much to look forward to and bargaining with God for good things. And he had given me good people.

And there was much to look forward to.

THE END

The Nightingale Files is purely a work of fiction though at times I have pulled on conversations, situations or locations that have existed.

The characters/schools/business are fictional and any representation of places or persons (living or dead) is coincidental.

Bentonville is a beautiful, real place, and we love living near it. I have not been compensated by the city itself or any business, mentioned or not, in the making of this book. However, if said institutions should like to sponsor the series going forward, I would gladly make mention of them.

Chess quotes were paraphrased from:

Yalom, Marilyn (2004), Birth of the Chess Queen: A History (2nd ed.), Perennial, ISBN 0-06-009065-0

Horton, Byrne J. (1959), Dictionary of modern chess, New York: Philosophical Library, p. 175, ISBN 0-8065-0173-1,

THE NIGHTINGALE FILES:
THE BISHOP AND PAWN

THE NIGHTINGALE FILES:
THE BISHOP AND PAWN

1.

A BAD BISHOP, PASSIVELY PLACED, CAN STILL HAVE USEFUL DEFENSIVE FUNCTION

"You're the one who got me into this. You can't flake on me now," I said into the phone pinned between my cheek and my shoulder as I laced up my shoes.

"I know, I know," Felix admitted with thick protest. "I just lack the proper motivation today," he joked.

"I'll give you twenty-four minutes to find it."

He laughed. "Why not seventeen?"

"Because it will take me twenty-four to run to your house."

"You're going to run to my house and then do our normal run too?"

"What can I say, I have extra steam to blow off today," I said, sighing loudly as I tied the other shoe.

"Still haven't heard from Nate?"

"Nope."

"Alright. I'll be ready when you get here. Be careful."

"Will do. I'll bring my Glock," I said laughingly.

"Do you even know what a Glock is?"

"No."

"I didn't think so. Better get to poundin' pavement if you want to make it in twenty-four minutes!"

"On my way."

I locked the front door, stretched on the porch, and gave myself the length of the driveway before I started running. I wasn't as natural at running as Felix was; with his impossibly long legs and lean muscles, he glided down the asphalt like a freakin' gazelle. My legs were getting stronger, and I could tell they had power behind them to carry me, but they certainly weren't long by any stretch of the imagination.

My legs were warming up, and my strides felt easy, so I pushed my feet further as I turned off my street. My breaths were even and slow like Felix had been teaching me.

Sweat beaded on my brow and began to slowly roll down my neck. The late summer heat was getting sweltering earlier and earlier in the day. The sun washed out the cloudless sky and trained its sights on me with the intent of melting me before I reached Felix.

We only had a couple of weeks until school started, but it was borderline miserable outside. Which probably meant it was boiling in California where Nate was.

At the thought of Nate, I cranked up the music in my earbuds and drowned out my thoughts.

My frustration ruled my legs, and I pushed a little harder around the corner to Wellington Boulevard, which connected to Felix's subdivision. Two houses down, there were new foundations going in and frames going up.

As I jogged past, I saw a boy leaning against a small oak tree, taking a smoke break. His jelled red hair caught fire in the sunlight, and his ice blue eyes followed me down the street. I looked away just as he threw down his cigarette and pushed off the tree, heading in my direction.

Maybe I really do need that Glock, I joked to myself, tamping down some nervousness.

The boy jogged up beside me and said something I couldn't hear, which was probably best, I thought. I didn't slow down, but I took my right earbud out. "What?" I asked breathlessly.

He smirked at me, which made the glacier blue dance in his eyes. As I did my best not to judge him, I had to admit that, for a construction worker, he was really good-looking.

"I just said 'hey,'" he repeated. He kept up with me even in his work boots.

"Hey." I smiled politely at him.

"Where you off to in such a hurry?"

Mostly away from you, I sneered a little inside, but out loud, I said, "Over to a friend's house. He's helping me train."

"You look like you're doing fine on your own."

He observed me very openly. I let him see me roll my eyes. He was laying it on thick, but, oddly enough, I didn't feel threatened by him. And ever since Ace, I was hypersensitive to boys and their intentions.

He had freckles high on his cheeks and a square jaw that

clenched when he tried not to smile too big.

"Thanks," I said, "but don't you need to get back to work?"

The boy looked back over his shoulder and cursed, seeing that his attentions had taken him three blocks further than he must have intended. He started to jog back, away from me, and I giggled to myself.

Just before I cut across the street into Felix's subdivision, I heard him shout after me, "Will you come back this way?"

I laughed and lifted my arms up like I didn't know.

"Come back this way. I need to see you again!"

I smiled but knew I was far enough away that he couldn't see it. I put my earbuds back in and pushed my hardest all the way to Felix's driveway, where I could see him stretching.

Felix had returned at the end of the school year from his semester at the "lab," as he called it. When his parents had sent him away to get to the bottom of his so-called abnormalities, I hadn't been sure how he would come back. But after therapists, counselors, doctors, physiatrists, and even a pastor had confirmed to his parents what I already knew—that there was nothing wrong with Felix—they had backed off and begun to accept him.

But Felix himself had changed. Not that he'd ever seemed insecure, but he was now sure of himself, and he was focused. He'd gone out for the track team and convinced me to do it to. It was the outlet we both needed.

Nate had gone off to a prestigious football camp in California and hadn't called since he'd left. We hadn't exactly broken up when he'd left, but our status and security definitely eluding me now. So, every day, Felix and I worked out our problems on the asphalt.

Felix threw a water bottle at me as I stopped at the edge of the drive. "Twenty-two point four five. Nice, AB! Got a little pep in your step this morning?"

I smirked at the thought of the redhead. "Yeah. Guess so." I shrugged. "You got those stilts warmed up yet?"

He shoved me, then winced. "Oh, gross. You're sweaty."

"Listen, Felix," I said, snapping his name like a whip, "if you can't accommodate sweat, you are in the wrong sport, my friend."

"I can accommodate mine. Doesn't mean I like yours."

I swiped my hand across my neck and left a long streak down his arm.

"You're disgusting, Avery Brave."

"I'm disgustingly faster than you!" I said as I took off down the street.

"Oh, Nightingale. You're going to pay for that!" he shouted after me.

I knew I would. In about four strides, he would catch up to me and probably pass me, but the thrill I got out of teasing him spiked my adrenaline and coursed through my quads as I pushed them forward faster and faster.

I fully expected to be tackled at any second, thrown down into the grass and left in his dust. But it never came.

I kept sprinting. One block, two. I quickly looked behind to see Felix chasing me, on my tail, but he hadn't caught me yet. A stitch grabbed my side, and I doubled over, holding it.

Felix slapped my back as he caught me. "AB! I think you're in the wrong event! Where did that come from?"

Heaving the breaths out to try and expand my lungs far enough past the stitch to relieve it, I answered, "I have no idea."

"You had to be running a seven-minute mile! I had no idea you had that kind of speed in those squats li'l legs of yours."

"They are pretty close to the ground," I joked.

"I'm going to tell coach we have a new sprinter."

"Don't you dare."

"Why not?" he challenged.

"Because maybe it was a one-time deal. A fluke."

Felix eyed me suspiciously. "I doubt it."

"Maybe I don't want to be a sprinter, Felix," I pushed back.

"Okay, okay," he said, grasping my shoulders. "I'm sorry. I see I struck some sort of nerve. I'm not trying to push you. So, let's just run." He searched for a nod of agreement. "Okay?"

I nodded sheepishly, not knowing what nerve he had struck or what it meant. "Okay."

We ran seven miles at a good clip, me struggling to keep up with Felix's lengthy strides. We talked about lake plans and laughed about our favorite shows. We caught up on what was happening with Carol, and, by the time we'd solved all the world's moral problems, we were back at Felix's house.

"Do you want me to drive you home?" he asked.

"Nah, I'll walk back. I need to cool down so I'm not stiff for the lake tomorrow."

"You sure?"

"Yeah. I'll be fine. Want to swim later?"

"Yeah, let me shower, and I'll be over after lunch."

"Okay. See ya," I said, waving at him and walking back in the direction I'd come from.

When I neared the construction site, I found it deserted. No men, no trucks, no redhead. But nailed to the tree where he had been leaning and smoking, there appeared to be a note.

My aching, exhausted legs protested, but my curiosity enticed me across the street to the tree. Sure enough, it was a note.

It read:

To the Angel with Honey-Colored Hair

Then, it listed his phone number. He'd signed it MB.

I smiled to myself and ripped the note from the nail and continued back to my house. I debated whether to run this way tomorrow.

When I walked into the house, Mother was mid-conversation with someone on the phone. I poured myself a glass of water, trying to catch my breath, and listened in half-unintentionally.

"No. That's what she said. They were going to start taking in teenagers." She nodded and then shook her head in disbelief. "I know, it seems risky, and...okay, I wasn't going to use that word, but yes. But she says that they feel like God wants them to do this."

I watched her from the counter as she listened and bobbled her head from side to side in slight agreement and disagreement. Then, when she could listen no more, she held up a hand and said, "But Helen, I don't really think it's our place to make that call. Really, what we need to do is be helpful. Be there for them. Even if it goes wrong, we need to be there for them."

I had never heard my mother be so bold with one of her friends, and it surprised me. It made me smile behind my glass.

"Okay?" She waited for a response and then nodded. When she hung up the phone, she turned and smirked at me. "Were you listening?"

I smirked back. "Who is taking in teens?"

"The Holdens."

"Cool."

"Cool? No deep thoughts from Avery Brave today?"

"No. They have a big house. If they know teens that need a place, they should do it. Seems like good math to me."

She chuckled. "I suppose it does. How was your run with Felix this morning?"

"It was good. Farther, faster, stronger...the usual."

She shook her head and laughed again as I slipped off the stool and kissed her on the cheek.

"I need a shower. Are you headed out?"

"Yes, I'm leaving in about ten minutes. What are you doing today?"

"Felix is coming to swim, and then I don't know."

"Lazy summer days, huh? Would you mind bringing your laundry down?"

"Not at all. I'll call you if we end up going anywhere."

"All right, dear," she called after me as I skipped up the stairs. I peeled off the sweaty—now crunchy—running shorts, tank, and sports bra and checked my phone before hopping in the shower. No missed calls. No messages from Nate.

I cared; I wouldn't lie to myself and pretend I didn't. Nate had been like a fairytale prince for several months after the whole ordeal of last year. It had been bliss—if a high schooler can experience such a thing. And maybe that was the problem. It was a fairytale.

He'd started pulling away when school was out, right before he left for the summer. Carol and Felix thought it was in my head, but I knew on some level it wasn't. And now, the lack of communication was my proof. I took my snack out to the front porch and let my hair dry in the breeze as I swung gently on the porch swing, thinking back to the first time Nate and I had sat here together. I wasn't angry or even hurt. It wasn't like we'd broken up, but I certainly felt confused.

And what was more, the butterflies in my stomach this morning from the redhead had added to the confusion. Was I just feeling neglected? Did I still have feelings for Nate? Maybe I was just lonely and looking for attention.

All of my emoting was interrupted as I saw police cars pull in to the house two doors down from us. Lights on but sirens off. I stood up from the swing and leaned on the railing, curious to see what was about to go down. We lived in an affluent neighborhood where disturbances, trouble, or chaos of any kind were unheard of.

Two police officers got out of their cars and walked to the door. They disappeared inside, and, after several moments, I felt guilty for watching with a twinge of anxiety or the thought of a break-in or domestic issues in our neighborhood.

Thankfully, Felix pulled up just as I broke away from staring at the blue lights.

"What's going on over there?"

"No idea. They just pulled up."

"I heard there have been several break-ins around here lately."

"Really? I haven't heard anything."

"Yeah, seems to be some suspicion surrounding the construction crews."

"How so?" I asked, thinking of the redhead.

"Seems they all go on break, disappear, and, when they do...things tend to happen. Could be coincidence. Could be their MO."

"Well, detective Felix, in your professional opinion...," I teased.

"Shut up."

"Come on in. You need a snack or a drink? I'm still replenishing."

"Naw, I'm good."

"Okay, I'll go change. I'll just be a sec. You can go ahead and get in if you want."

"Okay."

I headed up to my room, still thinking about the police cars. I wondered to myself what was the worst thing it could be. "Murder," I answered aloud to myself in a film noir sort of way and then giggled.

I changed into my suit and hurried down the stairs. I took the long way out to the pool by way of the front door to see if the police cars were still there. My curiosity was revving high, and I knew something big was going on. When I rounded the house and opened the gate to the pool, Felix immediately started teasing me, which I expected.

"You went out to see the police cars, didn't you!?" he exclaimed.

"Maybe," I teased back.

"You're restless and nosy."

"I'm what? You better take that back!" I sassed back at him while taking off my towel and inching my way back to the fence like I was prepping to take off.

"Don't you jump on me, Nightingale, or you'll regret it."

"Then take it back."

"I can't. It's already out in the universe, sadly enough." He shrugged. "Plus, it's the truth."

"Oh yeah?" I said. I leaned behind the lounge chair and retrieved the extra-large water gun my dad had bought, whirled it around, and soaked Felix in the face and chest before he even saw it coming. He yelped out of surprise but then started yelling threats at me as he tried to run in the water toward the stairs. We both doubled over laughing at his ridiculous attempt to chase me.

But our laughter was cut off with a knock at the gate and a familiar voice. Felix shot me a look, and I motioned for him to stay put.

A message from Megan-

Thanks for reading The Nightingale Files. I hope you loved going back to school with Avery Brave this year. There's plenty more to come—so stay tuned.

If you loved this book, please pass it on. Better yet—buy a copy for a friend. The best way to support authors is to buy books. The second-best way is to recommend the book, pass it on, or tell the world how much you love Avery Brave and her many adventures with a book review.

I love writing books, but it's not all I do. I'd love for you to join me on all my other adventures as well.

Join me:
Instagram: @meganmeredithauthor
Facebook: @MeganMeredithAuthor
Blog: http://www.themeredithmusketeers.com

Much Love,
Megan

Made in the USA
Monee, IL
08 July 2026

56679423R00104